DEAD MAN CHRONICLE

DEAD MAN CHRONICLE

MARCO NAVARRO

Paperback: 978-1-63767-748-3
eBook: 978-1-63767-749-0
Library of Congress Control Number: 2022903223

This is a work of fiction.

Ordering Information:

BookTrail Agency
8838 Sleepy Hollow Rd.
Kansas City, MO 64114

Printed in the United States of America

Contents

AARON

I sat in the corner of the new house's living room, eyeing the clock as it ticked, counting down the seconds left for the next minute. The soft moonlight glinted on the porcelain skin of the teacup as I tilted it to see that it was empty before getting up off the old chair—the only object in the room and the clock on the wall in front of it. I turned all the lights off but saw that the clock read 3:30.

I had to get some sleep; I kept thinking. Jane and I had not yet finished moving into the new house, and I was here alone until tomorrow when Jane arrived from her parents' House up north, three days' ride from here. That information came into my mind as I went to the kitchen to place the cup in the sink before going to the bedroom. Then, as I passed the rooms in the hallway, I heard a sound. I stopped in the hallway and turned back to see the door open slightly to one of the rooms. The door creaked loudly, leaving a tiny crack in the doorway. I walked over and opened the door to find the room empty.

Standing at the doorway, I looked around the room and found nothing inside, so I stepped out and started to close the door. Hopefully, it wasn't rodents, I thought as I began to walk away, but then I heard another sound in the same room. I turned back to open the door to find the space empty again. Then I started to hear someone breathing. A quiet flow came from the corner across the room, shrouded in darkness. I stood in silence as my body tensed up. The room looked empty, but I was sure I could hear someone breathing. Something hid in the darkness of that corner. I took a step, and the dark moved. The wooden floor creaked loudly as a figure moved through the black.

"A soldier," a raspy voice sounded out of the darkness. "You should not be here," the stranger said.

I stammered, trying to speak, but something paralyzed me. I couldn't say a word or even move. I could only watch as a woman slowly stepped out of the darkness. Her pale, gray skin shone in the moonlight, appearing like a ghost. Long strands of thin hair loomed over her face as she stood straight and took short steps in my direction. I tried to move away but couldn't move at all, not even a finger.

The woman stepped into the light. The eyes of a corpse pierced through the dark, thin hairs. She pointed her finger at me and said, "You reek of death."

"This!" The woman hissed, raising her arms to show me her hands. "This is what they did to me."

The moon's light shone through her hands like branches through the ripped skin and exposed bone. Her hands burned the image into my brain.

"Why are you here?" The woman asked. "Do you know what they're going to do to you once they've found you?" she asked, drawing closer. She locked her pale eyes with mine, clenching my face. Her dead eyes were like a fog, gray and cold eyes without light.

"They'll come for you," the woman continued. "They'll kill you. Then, they will defile your corpse and throw you into the woods. They will come for you!"

I closed my eyes as the dead woman crept closer until her breath touched the side of my face before she laughed maniacally. Her shrieking laughter roared into my ears. The woman then shuffled back, still laughing. I was expecting she would try to kill me, but all she did was laugh until I opened my eyes and she was gone.

Morning came. I sat in bed and looked out the window, out to the woods surrounding the house, focusing on something in the distance. Someone was standing across the yard. I rubbed my eyes and looked closer, but there was nothing now, just trees again. I got out of bed and went to the bathroom to splash my face with cold water. I then turned to turn off the water and stared in the mirror. Something didn't feel right. Was it a dream? I thought. Something about whatever that woman was saying.

I hadn't dried off yet and leaned against the sink, dipping my head. My mind replayed it over and over. I needed to know what she was talking about; who was the woman talking about? Who are *they*? Who was she?

I closed my eyes and breathed deeply. I already had nightmares, and I wasn't looking to occupy my mind with more dread. Maybe I was anxious and needed time to adjust to the new house. I didn't want to dwell on it, so I opened my eyes. I then noticed a drop of blood in the sink.

I watched the droplet slide down before looking at my hands and face in the mirror to see that the blood wasn't mine. Then another drop splattered on the sink from above. Finally, I turned my head up slowly to see something I hoped I'd never see again.

I froze completely, looking up at a corpse nailed to the ceiling—blood dripping from his nose and mouth.

The corpse on the ceiling reminded me of the woman in my dream. Her crooked face and rotting teeth invaded my thoughts. The dead woman's mouth gaped wide open as she screamed with dread. My ears rang as images rushed through my mind, memories of my harrowing experiences, and the night I decided I would not hurt anyone again.

I covered my ears and groaned in pain, dropping to the floor, remembering the flames that consumed the bodies we left that night. The mindless yelling and rageful expression on the dead woman's face flooded my mind right before her body burst open and painted the walls with her entrails.

The corpse that was on the ceiling let out a soft breath. A quiet exhale made the ringing stop. Silence filled the bathroom, and I looked up and stared mindlessly at the rotting corpse to watch it split open, spilling a fountain of blood onto the bathroom floor. The blood showered over me as I covered my eyes and fell back, yelling in panic as the blood smothered my hands and my clothes. I opened my eyes to see the bathroom now covered in blood. The skin of my hands was no longer visible. All I could see was red. My hands shook, and I didn't know what to do. Then, finally, I heard the bedroom door open and quickly turned to look.

"Aaron?" Jane's voice sounded outside the bathroom, Her footsteps approaching. "Are you okay in there? I heard a scream."

I blinked and looked around. The bathroom was clean now, and the corpse wasn't there anymore. I stammered. My mind was trying to piece together what had just happened while also coming up with an explanation for why I was on the floor.

"I...I'm okay, honey. I just slipped." I kept looking around the bathroom to figure out what had just happened.

"Oh, Okay," Jane replied, opening the bathroom door. "Hey," Jane said, smiling before looking at me with confusion. "Are you all right?" Jane asked.

"Hey," I said back, smiling. I looked around me before I stood up. "I...uh was splashing water on my face. I spilled some on the floor," I explained to Jane.

Jane raised her eyebrows to say, "Okay, dear. Can you go outside and help me quick?" Jane asked. "I brought some stuff from my parent's house. We need to bring it inside, and the movers will bring the rest tomorrow."

"Sure....yeah, I'll be out in a minute, hon. Just going to clean up here."

"Thank you, love," Jane said before kissing me, stepping out of the bathroom, and closing the door behind her. I turned to the mirror as the door shut. My face was still wet. I stepped up to the sink again, my hands trembling as I opened the valve to wash my hands. I quickly dried off my hands and face.

I stepped onto the porch to find Jane sitting and reading her bible in the rocking chair. I approached and stood next to her. She looked at me and smiled before moving the red bookmark and closing the book.

"Hey," Jane said, removing her reading glasses.

"Hey. You left your bible downstairs?" I asked her.

"Yeah. I did a little reading while you were asleep."

"You didn't wake me up? I could've helped."

"It's okay. You looked so cute asleep. I'm not going to interrupt that. Not ever," Jane said, giggling.

I chucked and kneeled next to Jane.

"Oh, well, you weren't up too long?" I asked.

"No...but, Aaron, I have to ask you something," Jane said insecurely.

"What is it?" I placed my hand on her forearm.

"I'm kind of nervous about moving here. It's just that I've been living with my parents my whole life, and this is a big step for me. For us, you know?"

"Well, I...." I didn't know what to say to Jane at that moment. My mind kept running back to what I had seen in the bathroom. Jane tugged on my hand, signaling me to sit with her. I didn't have an answer to what she was talking about. I stood up, and she moved to the side, letting me sit as I wrapped my arms around her and pressed her against me.

"You'll stay with me, right?" Jane asked.

"Always," I whispered.

Night came around. I sat in the living room again, staring at all the furniture we had yet to organize. My eyes burned from being up. I was afraid I'd see something again if I fell asleep. I looked at the clock; it was 4:00 in the morning. Moving here was a mistake; that was all I could think while I sat in silence, alone in the dark. A blank expression colored my face, but my thoughts raced, and something deep in my mind kept repeating one word,

"Run."

I headed upstairs and saw the light creeping out of the main bedroom. I kept my eyes on the door to the room and felt the atmosphere become heavier before hearing a creak from the door. And I watched the door close slowly before slamming shut.

"Jane?" I asked loudly. There was no answer.

"Jane?" I asked again.

I moved down the hallway and tried the knob, but something locked it. I found it strange because the door of that room had a broken lock. I pushed against the door and kept trying to open it, but it wouldn't budge. I shook the doorknob aggressively, but nothing was happening.

"Jane?.... Jane!" I called out, slamming my shoulder against the door until finally, the door flew open, and I stumbled into the room, but it wasn't our bedroom.

I was surrounded by a thick fog that concealed everything around me. I turned to the door behind me as it began to close and slammed shut.

"Hey!" I exclaimed, running at the door, which began to fade away until it finally disappeared. I looked around and found that the fog was starting to thin, and I could see what was in front of me.

The sky and the ground beneath collided with each other. The area was painted gray and black, forming the grim image before me.

The ground crunched as I stepped forward on the black rocks covering the whole area. The air was cold, but the ground under me was hot, and the whistling air sent a chill down my spine as I began to hear music from afar. The soft strumming of what sounded like a harp filled the air. I followed the music and the fog dissipated until I saw a figure sitting on a chair in the distance. The figure was dressed in black, and its head was covered by a hood.

It sounded as if the stranger was the one playing the harp. I took a step forward, and the ground began crunching, making the music stop. The figure slowly turned its head, and I could see its face staring back at me.

The stranger's face was like a man's but mangled and deformed. The strange man formed a grin under his white, milky eyes, revealing his blackened teeth. Large gashes covered his face as if someone had put him through a meat grinder.

I noticed a crown that sat atop the deformed man's head; the crown was rusty and covered in grime and large cavities that I assumed were for precious stones, but dirt now filled them. The mangled man kept his gaze fixed on me, and a voice in my head spoke, a demonic voice that whispered,

"I'll be seeing you soon, Aaron."

I stumbled back as the stranger filled the air with demonic laughter. I turned to run away, but my feet started to sink into the ground. The black rocks consumed me until I was in complete darkness.

I woke up in bed. I moved my arm across the other side of the bed where Jane should've been, but she wasn't there. I sat up to block the sunlight that poked through the window, blinding me. Jane wasn't in the room, so I quickly put on some clothes and went downstairs to look for her.

I could hear the graphophone playing in the kitchen. I walked over and recognized the melody playing; it was the same song the stranger played in my dream. I stopped and stood at the entrance of the kitchen. As the music continued, I went blank and felt my mind sinking into the dark again. Then I looked at Jane. She was standing at the stove. Jane braided her hair the only way Jane knew how to do it, and she was wearing her favorite dress underneath the apron her grandmother gave her.

Jane smiled when she saw me standing behind her. She wiped her hands with the dishcloth and walked over to me as she took my hands and pulled me towards her.

"Dance with me," Jane said, chuckling.

I let Jane pull me as she began to step back and forth, dancing to the music. She held my hand as she twirled and spun around with glee. She chuckled playfully before embracing me, and I wrapped my arms around her and kissed her head. She broke the embrace and walked to the stove. "I made breakfast," she said. "Are you hungry?"

"....Yeah," I said.

"Are you okay? You look like you saw something." Jane turned away to remove the apron and place it on the counter.

"....I."

I didn't know what to say. Jane noticed how distraught I was and told me to sit at the table as she took the eggs and bacon from the pan inside the stove and moved them to a plate before setting it on the table along with a coffee mug. She then took a bottle of milk from the refrigerator and some silverware from the drawer and put those on the table, too. She sat across from me and unfolded the bible on the table.

I took the coffee pot and the sugar she had already placed on the table and poured the coffee, sugar, and milk into the mug. I cocked an eyebrow as I took a sip of the coffee, and Jane looked at me from behind the book she was reading. I couldn't keep a straight face, so I started grinning, and Jane smiled back. We both sat there looking at each other. Finally, Jane stopped looking at me and stood up. Jane placed the book next to my breakfast as she sat on my lap and put her arms on my shoulders.

"So, what do you wanna do today?" she asked me.

"I don't know," I said, kissing her arms. "Did you have something in mind?" I asked.

"Well, I thought we could ride into town and maybe go sightseeing."

"Sightseeing? Don't we have to bring in the stuff the movers are bringing?"

"Yeah, but I don't want to be cooped up here all day. So I figured we'd get to know the town we're living in."

"How about I fire in the backyard and go hunting for some foul?"

"You want to spend all day in the woods looking for something to eat? We could just go into town and buy from the market."

"I guess we could do that."

Jane noticed that I wasn't engaged in the conversation.

"What's wrong?" Jane asked.

"I....I don't feel so good about coming here. I think we should...."

"We should what, Aaron?"

"....I think we should leave."

"You wanna leave? We just moved here." Jane said, standing up. She shifted over to the counter.

"I just.... I can't be here, Jane. I feel like I'm losing my mind. The past two nights, I've woken up to a different nightmare. There's something wrong with this demented house!"

Jane pressed up against the counter, crossing her arms.

"Are you suggesting we up and leave?" Jane asked. "What am I gonna tell my parents? That the house they gave me is haunted? I know you've seen some horrible things in your past, Aaron, and you can't sleep at night because of it, but you need to give me a good explanation here."

"Jane, I'm just trying to look out for us." I stood up from the chair but stayed where I was as I said, "I understand you can't trust what I'm saying, and I know the things I've seen in my past have caused you trouble. But, please, I need you to trust me."

"No, Aaron," Jane said, "I love you, but I don't want you to worry anymore about who you used to be. You can't keep letting the past affect you, Aaron. So we moved into this house, and we're staying." Jane threw her apron against the sink, turning away from me to rest against her hand on the counter.

I sighed and cleared my throat before walking to Jane to hug her from behind. She took my hand, squeezed it tightly, then turned and kissed my cheek to hug me. I wanted to explain to her what was happening, but I didn't know how to.

"I'll bring the rest of the furniture in," I uttered. "When are the movers getting here?"

Jane turned her head away from me to finish washing before rubbing her hands under the faucet and drying them off. Then she walked to the radio to turn down the volume and collect the plates with the unfinished breakfast I had left. I stood still to look at Jane before going upstairs to the bedroom to get two cigarettes from my cigar box. random items filled the box. Items that I had forgotten about or had no use for; old war medals and patches from my regiment and a red feather; something that brought back a horrible memory. I noticed something interesting buried underneath all of it; a picture of Jane and me at our wedding. She had the biggest smile, and I had the usual expressionless look on mine.

I took the photo and placed it in my pocket with the cigarettes before putting the box back in the drawer and leaving the room. I walked out onto the porch, closing the door behind me. I took a cigarette from my pocket and put it between my lips. I checked my bags for matches, but I couldn't find any. I groaned in frustration and turned around to go back inside, but as I reached for the door, I noticed something moving at the side of the house. I stepped off the porch and saw a figure move into the backyard.

"Hey!" I called out to the figure, but it slipped away.

I walked to the backyard and saw the stranger walking toward the forest. He was covered by a cloak that reached down to his feet. I couldn't see who it was. The figure strode slowly towards the woods right before I stopped it by getting its attention.

"Hey!" I called out.

The figure stopped and slowly turned around to face me. It was a young man who was no older than I was when I joined the army. The young man looked at me. He stared at me without an expression on his face, and then he grinned. The young man removed the hood of his cloak and revealed his silver hair and pale skin. He looked made of ice, staring coldly with dead, frosted eyes.

"It's finally nice to meet you, Aaron," the young man said.

"How do you know my name?" I asked.

The young man chuckled before answering, "You'd be surprised what I know about you," he said boastfully. "Tomahawk."

I was paralyzed by what he said. How could he have known to call me that? I thought.

"Why did you say that name?" I asked.

"That is what they called you, isn't it? 'Tomahawk?' Seventeen confirmed kills, all done with a hatchet and a service pistol. You have quite a reputation, Aaron. Not to mention the horrible things you've done to people who.... well, deserved it. I wonder who else knows about that."

I took two steps forward and yelled, "You better explain what you're doing here! Who are you?"

The young man's grin grew more prominent. He was unthreatened by what I said. He stood still, keeping his cold, dead eyes fixed on me from where he was standing. I could feel my blood beginning to boil.

"I'm not here to hurt you, Aaron. This is simply a warning."

"Warning from what?" I asked. I balled my fists and repositioned myself. I was expecting this kid to attack, but he didn't.

"They're on their way now," A voice sounded inside my head. "I suggest you start running.... Fast."

"Who are you!" I demanded.

The young man grinned again as he hissed out his name, "I'm Asmodeus."

I looked at him fiercely. What could he have meant? Who was coming?

The young man turned to the forest and covered his head with the cloak before smiling back at me. His mouth didn't move, but I was sure that I heard his voice in my head saying,

"They'll be here soon."

Asmodeus disappeared into the woods. I dropped the cigarette still in my hand and ran back into the house to find Jane.

"Jane!" I called out. She was no longer in the kitchen, so I looked upstairs.

"Jane?" I called again.

"Downstairs!" Jane responded.

I headed to the basement and found Jane organizing boxes.

"Did you bring all this stuff down by yourself?" I asked.

"No," Jane replied. The movers came early in the morning, and you were still sleeping, so I told them to bring everything down here. I figured I could get started and organize some of the small stuff on my own."

I blanked out. Asmodeus' voice whispered words that reverberated in my head. The image of an old friend appeared as I flashed back and saw my friend's hand reaching out to me as he handed me his hatchet, saying,

"This will protect you, Aaron."

My name was repeated over and over,

"Aaron.... Aaron?.... Aaron!"

I blinked and looked at Jane.

"Did you even hear what I said?" Jane's voice was filled with contempt.

"I...."

Jane scoffed.

"Aaron, what the hell is going on?" She asked.

I was going to explain to Jane all the horrible things happening in the house, but I was interrupted by the sound of someone knocking on our door.

Jane and I looked at each other in confusion.

"Who is that?" Jane asked.

"I don't know," I said. "Stay here."

I went back upstairs to the front door and looked out the window to see three men standing on our porch. The one closest to the door had his back turned. The other two were facing the door. I twisted the doorknob and opened the door to stand before the three men. The one closest to the door turned to face me. He was very tall and wore a large-brimmed fedora covering the top half of his face, so I could only see his scruffy stubble and the black of his outfit. The man in black reached over his head to remove his hat.

"Afternoon," the man in black said, smiling.

"Hi," I replied. "Can I help you, gentlemen?" I asked.

"We're with the Sheriff's Department," the man in black answered.

"Sheriff's department?" I closed the door and stood outside with them on the porch. "Is something wrong?" I asked.

"We came down here because we're looking for a group of individuals. Outlaws that escaped from our jailhouse last night. We were wondering if you've seen anything that might point us in their direction. We normally don't go out this far, but these are some dangerous individuals. We need to find them quickly because they will hurt someone."

I was confused as I noticed none of them were wearing stars.

"Um, well, I haven't seen or heard anything. I'm new to this place. I just moved here with my wife. Got here yesterday."

"I see," Leonard said. "Well, congratulations, mister, um...."

"....Weller. Aaron Weller." I interrupted. "Pardon me, but who did you say you were?"

"Oh, I'm sorry, son," the man in black said, holding his hat up to his chest. "My name is Leonard Park. I'm the deputy chief." He then moved his hand to the right to introduce the men behind him. "This old fool is Sergeant Marvin Whissel, and this young man to my left is Philip. Uh...Philip young. He's a deputy."

The fellow to his right was heavy-set and shorter than Leonard and wore a fedora too. Philip was taller than Marvin but shorter than Leonard. He had patchy stubble and beady eyes. He was much slimmer and weaker than the other two, but I noticed something in their eyes. All of them had the same eyes.

"I see," I said to Leonard. "What county did you say you were from?" I asked.

"We're from Pine Stake. That's where we're stationed."

"I see, I said, slightly turning my body towards the door and placing my hand on the knob. I was about to turn the knob and go inside, but Leonard stopped me as he said,

"Son, It's over."

I tensed up, gripping the doorknob tightly. Leonard moved his coat, revealing the sidearm on his belt.

"Don't make this difficult," Leonard said.

I twisted the knob slowly so they couldn't hear it, and I threw open the door and ran inside the house, shutting it behind me.

"Aaron, is everything alright?" Jane asked, coming out of the kitchen.

The men outside tried to open the door as I tried blocking it. I yelled to Jane, "Run!"

"Aaron?" Jane asked worriedly.

The door burst open, and I was thrown across the floor. I stood up quickly and moved to grab Jane and heard a gunshot. I fell to my knees and saw blood on the walls. I felt someone grab the back of my head then I was forced down against the floor. I looked up at Jane and watched Leonard approach her.

"Don't you dare touch her!" I cried out before Marvin smashed my head against the floor. I groaned, still trying to fight my way out.

"I'm gonna kill you!" I yelled at the two men.

Leonard wasn't listening to me. Instead, he walked up to Jane, pressed his pistol against her chest, and fired.

"No!" I cried out.

Jane fell to the floor, and Leonard squatted in front of her. I fought harder to get out of their grasp, but I was powerless.

"All right," Leonard said as he stood back up and breathed. "Take him out back and shoot him once the others get here. Philip will dump him in the woods."

Marvin spoke to Leonard, saying, "You know, we could take him to...."

"....No," Leonard interrupted. "They're of no use to us. Besides, this one's not clean. He's got a lot of sins to pay for. Ain't that right, Aaron?"

"Gressil," Leonard said, looking at Marvin. "You go get the others. I'll stay here with him."

Leonard walked around us and put his foot on my back. He pressed against the wound on my back caused by Marvin's shotgun, and I groaned painfully. Finally, Marvin stood up, releasing me from his hold. I tried to move again, but Leonard's foot was heavy—I couldn't understand how I couldn't get out from under it.

Marvin stepped outside. I couldn't see where he had gone. The room fell silent as Leonard and I were alone now. Leonard took out his pistol and pulled out the shell casing he had used to put in a new bullet.

The shell hit the floor like a brass coin, bouncing against the wood and clanking loudly. The cylinder clicked as he revolved it to place the new bullet into the hole.

"You know, I once had that look," Leonard spoke. "The one you got on your face right now. I lost everything once, too, but in doing so, I realized that....none of this shit matters, and I know you understand that too. That's why you don't fear death, Aaron. You desire it." Leonard pressed his pistol against my temple and cocked back the hammer to shoot, but he didn't. Instead, he just stood upright and holstered the gun again as he chuckled sinisterly.

"We ain't through with you just yet." He muttered.

I looked around, trying to find something to help me break free. If he was keeping me alive, then it meant that something worse was coming. I needed to get out of here and find the weapons I buried in the forest. I needed to kill these guys for what they did to Jane. I needed to get out.

Leonard sighed and shifted his right foot forward, pressing his other foot harder against my back as he holstered his weapon when I noticed the knife in his boot. I slid my hand across the floor to reach the blade.

Leonard was startled by the vase that had fallen from the table by the entrance. He turned back to see the vase shattered on the floor. I reached out, took the knife from his boot, and stabbed it into his ankle.

Leonard shouted in pain, and I pushed him off me and ran for the door. Philip stood on the porch, and I tackled him off. We both hit the ground, slammed against the dirt before, stabbed him in the back, and ran off towards the woods. I could hear someone yelling in the distance behind me, saying,

"Get off your ass and give me a rifle!"

I then heard a gunshot, followed by the whizzing sound of a bullet flying past my head. Then another one.

I felt a sharp pain in my stomach before I stumbled to the ground. I forced myself to get up, but it made the pain worse. I was near the forest but knew I wouldn't make it. I lifted myself to walk and pressed my hand against my stomach. I could feel my hand warming up from the blood as it gushed out of the wound. The red liquid oozed through my fingers and dripped onto the grass beneath me. I then heard a rustling sound coming from the woods in front of me. A group of dark, cloaked figures stepped out from amongst the trees. They stood around me, forming a circle. Marvin stepped out from behind them.

Footsteps crept up from behind. Someone was making their way toward us. A man yelling in anger approached from behind. I could hear him getting closer. His footsteps sounded heavy and fast-paced. Leonard was coming up behind me. His voice exclaimed something angrily,

"You Goddamn mother...."

Leonard whacked me in the back with his rifle, and I fell forward against the grass, blacking out for a brief moment.

I woke up again when I felt someone kick me hard in the stomach.

"That's good enough, Leonard," another voice interrupted. Asmodeus stepped out from the forest through the hooded figures. A grin formed across his face as he approached.

"He's suffered enough," Asmodeus muttered. "It's time we put him out of his misery."

"You," I hissed.

Asmodeus adjusted my shirt collar as he replied,

"Look at you, Tomahawk. I told you what would happen if you didn't leave, yet here we are."

"What the fuck did you do, Asmodeus?" My speech was slurred; I was losing a lot of blood.

Asmodeus stood upright and looked down at me as he replied,

"I've freed you. You should be thanking me."

I looked at him and said, "You…. don't know….what you've done."

I coughed blood after speaking. I was starting to check out. Asmodeus looked at Leonard and gave him a nod, and at that moment, I realized it was over. I lost Jane. She was everything to me and had been the only good thing in my life, and now I, too, was about to die. All I wanted was to have someone I could trust, but I should have realized that Jane could not trust me. I swallowed my blood and looked up at the sky.

"Forgive me," I whispered.

I then felt the cold steel of a gun press against the side of my head. The gun clicked as Leonard cocked back the hammer. I reached into my pocket and crumpled the photo I had. I closed my eyes and gritted my teeth as I felt the gun press harder against my head. The shot echoed, and my eyes didn't open again.

DEATH

I woke up in darkness. I moved my eyes around, scanning the area to see where I was. I moved my arms to pick myself up but felt something blocking me from standing up. I felt something creep through my fingers, something that felt like dirt. I moved my hand up to my chest, forcing it through the dark obstruction.

I forced my hand through the dirt until I felt nothing blocking it, finally reaching the surface. I pulled myself up from under the ground, and the soil crumbled around me as I escaped from the shallow grave. I rolled over, looked at the sky above, and saw the tall trees surrounding me—I was in the forest.

I looked down and noticed blood stains and holes in my shirt. I poked my fingers through the holes and felt scars on my stomach.

I whispered something when I looked under my shirt to find bullet wounds, "What the f....?"

"....Hello, Aaron."

I turned quickly to see who had said that. A young man stood across from me. I stood up quickly to attack but promptly fell to the ground, groaning in pain with my hand pressed against my stomach.

The young man stepped forward and reached out his hand, and I had a brief flashback to a moment I had just like this.

"Who are you?" I asked, taking the young man's hand.

"I understand you had an unfortunate run-in with some miscreants." The young man replied as he pulled me up.

"What the hell are you talking about?"

"I'm Gabriel," the young man answered. "Do you know what happened to you?" He asked.

I took a moment to examine Gabriel. He seemed young. He was a tall, blonde kid wearing a long, brown leather coat that almost reached his feet with a hexagonal patch on the shoulder of his jacket. Gabriel seemed like the military type, but his uniform was not one I recognized.

"Not sure. I woke up buried under the ground. I don't know how I ended up in this place," I answered.

"Someone murdered you and your wife," Gabriel said.

I walked past Gabriel to lean against a tree, each step hurting like hell. Finally, I leaned back and slowly sat down.

"And how do you know that?" I asked Gabriel.

"I saw it happen."

I looked down at the ground and sighed deeply.

"And you didn't do anything to stop it?" I asked.

"I couldn't," Gabriel replied.

"Really? Why's that?" I asked.

"It's complicated, Aaron, but if you come with me, I can explain."

"You better have a good explanation, pal. I'm having trouble understanding just what the hell happened to me."

"You're dead, Aaron."

I looked up at Gabriel. I wasn't sure what he meant.

"What makes you say that? Who are you?" I asked him.

"I'm here to help you."

"Why should I believe that?"

Gabriel turned to me and said, "Because I'm all you got."

I hesitated for a moment. "You mean to tell me that-"

"...Yes," Gabriel interrupted. "Someone murdered you."

"Why?" I asked.

"There is a lot that you still don't understand, Aaron. But if you're willing, I can help you rectify this."

"Rectify what? I don't know why I'm dead!"

"You don't?...." Gabriel stammered.

"Don't what?" I asked.

"....Nevermind. Is there anything you do remember?"

"Just my ghosts."

"What are you talking about?" Gabriel asked.

"It's a long story," I replied.

Gabriel didn't say anything. He just stood there looking at the ground with a blank stare.

"I don't know what you want from me. Just tell me why I'm here," I demanded.

Gabriel's eyes darted in my direction.

"Aaron, what I am offering you doesn't.... happen. I shouldn't be doing this, but I need your help."

"You need my help?" I asked

Gabriel sighed. "It's a very complicated situation, but I need to ask you if you are prepared to take on what's ahead."

I looked down and took a breath. Then, my eyes shot up to look at Gabriel.

"After what I've seen? I'm more than capable." I stated.

"Then follow me, Aaron," Gabriel said, walking away from where I was sitting. "We don't have any time to waste."

I stood and forced myself to walk with Gabriel. He led me through the woods but never said where he was taking me. Finally, Gabriel stopped, and I asked where he was taking me.

"Step in," Gabriel said, pointing at the rectangle.

I took a deep breath.

"This is gonna be a doozy," I said. I stopped in front of it and looked at Gabriel. He nodded. I groaned and took a step in.

I walked into a massive room constructed of pearlescent marble and decorated with two large sets of stairs next to each other, each made of sparkling gold, and in between were two large wooden doors.

Gabriel stepped through the magical doorway and approached the two wooden doors to open them. He signaled me to follow him, and I looked around to admire the place as I did.

"What the hell are you? And What is this place?" I asked, looking around.

"This is the spirit house. Raphael and I have been using this as a base of operations."

"Uh-huh. Who's Raphael?" I asked, still looking around, finally stepping up to the doors but admiring the room.

"I'll introduce you in a second. But, first, I need to explain our mission and why we chose you," Gabriel waited for me to follow him down the hallway past the doors. I finished perusing the gorgeous entrance and followed him.

"What is this?" I asked as we approached a set of doors in the corridor.

"This is a room that I created. But, unfortunately, I had not found a good use for it until now."

"Okay," I muttered.

Gabriel opened the door and stepped in. "So," he said. "the men that murdered you are not human."

"Then what are they?" I asked, looking around. The room was empty and void of any sort of object.

The room was just an empty marble structure made up of four sides; walls, floor, ceiling, and a series of rectangular windows across the border on the other side of the room, allowing light to enter.

"Demons," Gabriel replied.

I approached the windows to see outside and found nothing, just an empty, gray space that looked like we were inside a cloud.

"You're serious?" I said, looking out the window.

"Yes, and they're crossing into your dimension. Can you guess as to why that'd be troublesome?" Gabriel asked. I think he was being rhetorical.

"I.... I don't know, Gabriel," I said as I finally turned to look at him.

"They want to destroy you all."

"All of whom?" I asked as I walked over to where Gabriel was standing

"Humanity."

"That's.... A lot. What do I have to do with any of this?"

Gabriel looked at me to answer my question.

"You're invisible," another voice interrupted. I looked at the doors and saw a man standing at the room's entrance. Footsteps echoed as the shadowy figure approached. A tall man stepped into the light. A man with Black hair and a beard. Tall and broad, unlike Gabriel, who was leaner.

"Who is this?" I asked Gabriel.

"Aaron," Gabriel answered, "this is Raphael."

"So," Raphael said, "You're Aaron Weller."

I looked straight into Raphael's eyes as he walked up to Gabriel and me. He seemed very intense in the way he was looking at me.

"My name is Raphael. I am an archangel."

I looked at him awkwardly, cocking an eyebrow. "Is that supposed to mean something?" I asked blatantly.

"Did Gabriel explain to you why you're still alive?" Raphael asked.

"Hm, I don't feel alive," I said obnoxiously. Raphael didn't react to what I had said. Instead, he just stood there looking at me.

"Aaron, I need you to understand something. The only reason you're alive is that someone had mercy on you. I know what you are and the things you've done, and believe me, this is a far better deal."

"Okay," I said, "So, I'm an asshole. What do you want from me?"

"We don't want anything from you," he said. "We just need you to do something for us. You'll help us take down the ones who killed you."

"Why?" I asked.

"Because my job here is to find a way to deal with the situation. You are something that we just aren't, A human. Demons are beginning to cross into your dimension, and that's going to become a huge problem, and Gabriel and I can't get close to Lucifer."

"Why not?" I asked in confusion.

"Lucifer is a fallen angel. He is cursed, but he was once one of us. Which means he can detect us when we're near."

"So, what? I mean, you guys are angels. Why do you need me? I'm just a human."

"Yes," Raphael said.

"Won't he be able to detect me, too?" I asked.

"Not if you're dead," Gabriel replied.

"We need you to find his physical form, and we'll take care of the rest, but first, you'll have to take out his captains. That'll weaken his power, and it'll force him to come out of hiding," Raphael explained.

"How's that?" I asked.

"Lucifer relies on certain points of control," Gabriel answered. "These are areas that contain concentrated power, which Lucifer feeds on. Therefore, he. He needs these areas to be operational at all times to consume power."

"And how does he gain power from these control points? What's his power source?" I asked.

Gabriel and Raphael exchanged looks then they both looked at me. They didn't want to say it.

"He's using humans as a resource," Raphael stated.

"What do you mean?" It was unclear from his answer, and I was confused as to why they didn't want to say.

"....He drinks human blood to gain power, Aaron," Gabriel answered.

I sighed deeply.

"This is insane," I said under my breath.

"If there were a better way, we would use it." Instead, Gabriel said, "but we don't have time, Aaron. You're all we got."

I still didn't fully understand the situation, and they weren't giving me any choice, but if what they say is true, that I was dead and the only way to find out what happened to me was to do this for them, then I had to. I had to know the truth.

"Fine," I muttered, "I'll do it."

"Good," Raphael replied. "Then it's time we showed you your enemy.

The room's light dimmed, and the image of six people stood before us: five men and one woman. Raphael started from left to right, explaining who these people were. I looked at the images that had appeared before us. These people seemed to be standing in the room with us.

Raphael walked over to me and pointed his finger at the figures, saying,

"The first one to the left is Gressil. He's temperamental, unstable, and extremely dangerous. Next in line is Balberith The Blasphemer. He's a very well-trained swordsman and is a master of torture and interrogation. Next to him is Rosier. She commands an army called the sons of the earth. We have only seen a handful of her soldiers in battle, but they are fierce and violent creatures."

"The one next to her is our man himself, Lucifer, the father of lies, the prince of darkness, and the ruling emperor of Hell," Raphael explained.

"How are you doing that?" I asked.

"It's a reflection, and don't ask me to explain how it works," Raphael said. "Lucifer has other high-ranking individuals that handle his more sensitive matter."

The image of a man dressed in a black outfit appeared before us.

"Leonard is a warlock who specializes in black magic and darkness," Raphael explained, "and he is the person who summoned them."

"What about Asmodeus?" Gabriel asked.

Another image appeared before us.

"Asmodeus is one of the seven princes of Hell. He is deceitful and clever, and he's ruthless. So do not underestimate him." The way Raphael spoke of Asmodeus made it seem personal.

"All right," I said firmly.

"On to the next one," Raphael said. "Here we have Astaroth, The Great Duke of Hell. He is mighty, and he rules over Hell alongside Lucifer. He is the commander of an army of darkness called The Twelve Shadows."

Astaroth had a similar appearance to Lucifer, but he looked older and angrier. Lucifer's eyes looked filled with hate, but Astaroth's eyes had something more focused: vengeance.

"Next, we have Sonneillon, the demon of hatred," Gabriel stated. "He is your next target." Sonneillon looked different from the others. He was a pale-skinned man with long black hair, much like Raphael's, but his hair was curly and ungroomed. His face looked as if it had been painted white, with black paint surrounding his eyes. His pale skin was made more apparent by the black jacket he was wearing, along with the skin of his chest and torso, as he was not wearing a shirt with his jacket's sleeves rolled up.

"He's not a powerhouse like Lucifer or Astaroth," Raphael said, "nor is he a gifted fighter like Balberith, and he doesn't command an army like Rosier, but he is stubborn and doesn't like losing. So be careful with him."

"Sure," I said. "So, how do I take these guys down?"

"Follow me," Raphael instructed.

❋

BLOOD

Asmodeus

I awoke in a small bed crafted out of wood. The mattress was too small for the bed frame. I remembered where I was. I was in an old shack outside of a small town. I knew this because I could smell it.

I wasn't feeling well about coming to a place like this as I realized the shack didn't have much for me to use as I was preparing everything to head out and get to where I needed to go. Also, I was still unfamiliar with the experience of being so far away from where I usually am, and all I knew was that the person who sent me here was waiting for me.

I stepped outside and found Two men sitting outside on horses. I looked right at them and asked,

"When did you guys get here?"

"This morning," one of them replied. "Boss wanted us to give you a lift. He said you spawned too far from the destination."

"I was going to scout the location first," I hissed back.

"No need," The other rider replied.

I was confused by the rider's statement, but considering the time pressure, I had to take their word for it.

"Let's go then," I said.

One of the riders dismounted his horse as I approached.

"Let's move," I said, speeding down the snowy hill. The town was visible in the distance, just past the woods. There it was. Black Rose.

Three people were standing outside the woods watching the town and several of our soldiers waiting in the forest.

I dismounted from my horse and approached the three captains. Rosier, Gressil, and Leonard.

"Well, it's about time you showed," Leonard said.

"This is where we will summon our master," I stated. "Everyone is ready?"

"All according to your plan," Gressil replied.

"Good. Once we've taken it, we'll need fuel to summon our master. We'll also need enslaved people, so gather the women and the children. Everything else can burn."

"Sounds good to me," Leonard said, placing his rifle over his shoulder.

"Let's get moving then," Rosier said, "We don't want to keep *him* waiting any longer."

Leonard stepped forward with Gressil. The army of demons behind us crept out of the forest, hundreds of soldiers armed and ready to bring chaos.

Rosier mounted her horse and moved behind Leonard and Grissel as I walked alongside her. Riders on horses passed us by, rushing towards the town, following Gressil. Rosier went with Leonard, and I made my way to enter a saloon with a group of subordinates. I sat at an open table as my soldiers spread across the bar. Everyone was staring at us.

"What can I get for you, mister?" A young waitress approached my table.

I looked up at her, sitting in my chair, and gave her a sinister smile as I said,

"We're going to kill everyone in here." I waved my finger around.

The waitress froze up.

"What the hell did you say, boy?" A man's voice sounded from behind me as a customer stood up from his chair, coming up behind.

"You got a lot of nerve coming in here and saying something like that," The man continued. He was tall and looked strong, but he wasn't ready.

I felt his hand grip my shoulder, and I turned to him, quickly getting up from the chair, revealing the sword I concealed under my cloak. The blade impaled his stomach. I looked at him and watched as he started to die. The barkeep aimed a rifle in my direction before his head exploded from a bullet.

The unarmed civilians ran out into the street as we started killing everyone in the tiny, little saloon. They ran away from the massacre, but there was more outside, and they only ran to their deaths.

Gunshots sounded outside the saloon as civilians were dying in the street. I stepped outside and watched my soldiers drag civilians out into the road to execute them without mercy, all day and all night. I watched them burn down entire buildings filled with people. My master would've been proud of the brutality we were displaying, but this was just a tiny step toward what we had planned for them, for the world.

By morning the town was layered with a thick fog. I rode upon a horse, heading deeper into Black Rose. Rosier rode next to me as we went to the town square to a chapel. Our soldiers awaited our arrival with a group of townspeople gathered outside, bonded with ropes.

"Is this all of them?" I asked with contempt.

"Sir," one of the soldiers replied, "You asked to gather the ones with the "special" blood; this is what is left." The soldier pointed to the humans.

"Such filth," I muttered, looking at the town.

I looked at a group of women. They trembled as the cold wind crept across the entrance of the chapel.

"Well, let's get started then. I want these children taken to the black rooms. Take the adults down to the corridors, and prepare the altars in the chamber. We'll begin the ritual once they've been cleaned and dressed for their ascension."

The soldiers followed my orders and led the people into the chapel. The children entered first with Rosier, and my subordinates led the women inside. I walked down the church hall to the front, where a black doorway stood open, waiting for us to enter. A tall, black rectangle stood in the center of the church's altar.

"Step into the portal," I instructed.

The pitiful humans were hesitant until I pulled the rope that tied them together. Then, they finally stepped in and exited the earthly dimension.

A few moments had passed as I wandered the black corridors, making my way to the room where we kept the sacrifices. I opened the room door and found the women prepared for the ritual. Now dressed in white linen and their bodies cleansed. I entered the room quietly and explained to them the privilege they were about to receive by becoming sacrifices to our Lord.

"All of you have been chosen to bring a new era of glory and triumph. You are the children of the Lightbringer. You are the lamb. Take this step to become the sacrifices for our divine conqueror, do not fear. You will be delivered soon. Now, follow me."

My subordinates prepared the sacrifice room and cleaned the altar. Then, I directed the sacrifices to their positions where they would have their turn to ascend. They were blindfolded, and I took the first sacrifice and led them to the altar.

"Let us begin," I instructed.

I waved my hand to have cloaked figures appear next to each sacrifice. More figures entered the room. Women wearing black veils that covered their faces directed them to the altar and placed shackles on their ankles and wrists.

The women in the black veils stepped up to the altar and took a knife from their sleeves.

I then whispered, "Praise be the dark lord."

The women in the black cloaks shouted in unison,

"All hail Lucifer!" as they raised their blades into the air and shoved their knives into the first sacrifice. The sacrifice shook and fought to break the chains as their blood showered the altar before stopping and lying still. The blood then spilled onto the floor, flowing through the cracks of the base of the altar.

Leonard

After the fog and the smoke had cleared, I found Rosier strolling through the town on her horse, making her way to the chapel in the town square. The stench of death crept into my nostrils, with the streets littered with human corpses. Rosier looked satisfied. She passed by me on her horse, smiling at me, and I followed her. Rosier dismounted her horse, and we entered the chapel.

I followed Rosier through the hall to the altar, where she waved her hand in the air, and a black doorway appeared before us. We stepped through the portal into a long corridor Rosier, and I walked through until we reached a set of tall, black doors. Rosier and I stopped before the doors and stood in wait.

The sound of the doors opening echoed down the hall. Then, finally, the loud rumbling of the massive doors opening shook the corridor.

We were now in Lucifer's chamber, which was twice as big as the chapel I saw before. A series of steps led down to the floor that was colored red, surrounded by black marble. A single light floated in the darkness that hung above. The altar was located at the other end of the room and constructed of the same black marble, like a negative image of the chapel above.

Rosier walked up to the edge of the black steps to meet Asmodeus. A tall, black throne sat across the room on the altar.

Asmodeus stepped down and stood in the center of the room, facing south.

He placed his hands down and dipped them into the floor as the floor became liquid.

Asmodeus began to whisper something in the angelic language, and the floor began to form a cutout in the shape of a triangle. The triangle sunk into the floor like a pool, and the red fluid began filling the cutout.

The red color of the floor changed to black as the pool filled up.

The blood flowed around Asmodeus, wetting his cloak and filling the pool. Asmodeus signaled something to Rosier, so she led a group of children into the room. The children were carrying a deformed body. They moved down the entrance steps and held the body over the pool of red fluid. Asmodeus stood up and silenced himself. He nodded, and the children tossed the body into the blood pool before moving to each point of the triangle.

The red fluid splashed as the body sunk into the blood until it was no longer visible. Asmodeus raised his arms into the air and cried out,

"In nomine Dei nostri Satanas Luciferi excelsi!"

The blood began to bubble and vaporize as it started to boil. Then, the blood began to move violently like a raging sea until it shot up into the air like a geyser. The red fluid splashed everywhere, dousing everyone in the room, and once it had stopped, a man appeared in the center of the room, kneeling before them.

"Master," Asmodeus said as he dropped to his knees and bowed before Lucifer. Rosier and I did the same.

Lucifer stood up and grinned, covered in blood, as he muttered, "Well, it was about damn time."

Lucifer stretched out his arms. The children surrounding him washed away the blood from his skin with towels. They then placed a long, black robe over his shoulders. The cloak looked tattered and torn up. Lucifer stepped to the throne and sat down as the enslaved children exited the room.

Rosier and Asmodeus fell to their knees and bowed to Lucifer. Then, Asmodeus directed the children out of the chamber before making his way to Lucifer's throne.

"My master," Asmodeus said as he kneeled before Lucifer and kissed his hands.

"My dear Asmodeus, I hope everything I left to you is going according to plan."

"Yes, of course. Who else could you trust with such an important mission, my lord? I pledged myself only to you, and I will carry out your command without fail. I–"

"...My lord, I need to know what your next step is," Rosier interrupted Asmodeus as she approached Lucifer.

Asmodeus seemed troubled, but Lucifer did not acknowledge Asmodeus's feelings. Instead, Lucifer turned his attention to Rosier as she continued to speak.

"My servants are growing impatient. Sonneillon has become divergent and no longer wants to do his part for our cause. I need to know what you plan to do. Next, Lucifer, So I can get my forces in line."

Lucifer sat back against his throne.

"Rosier, do not grow weary. Tell Sonneillon that I have arrived, and we will celebrate my arrival. Remind Sonneillon that he is a part of this and tell him that if he doesn't want to serve my purpose, you will rip out his heart with your hands and serve it to me on a plate! Go now."

Rosier bowed to Lucifer and hurried out of the chamber.

"Is something wrong, Master?" Asmodeus asked Lucifer, walking up the steps of the altar.

"You noticed?" Lucifer asked.

"I noticed the look on your face. What do you need of me, my lord?"

"I'm not certain," Lucifer said. "Something I need to confirm. Leonard, follow Rosier. Keep a close eye on her," Lucifer said to me.

I nodded and bowed to Lucifer before walking away and leaving the room.

Asmodeus stood next to Lucifer and began washing away the blood on Lucifer.

"In the meantime, I want you to go to Astaroth. He has requested your presence."

"What does he want?" Asmodeus asked. He seemed bothered.

"Astaroth wants you to conduct his final ritual. I do not trust him, but if he is not against us, we need to keep him on our side."

The last of Lucifer's words echoed out into the corridor as the doors closed behind me.

I tracked Rosier and watched as she came out of the woods on her horse. She was looking at a house that was in the distance.

A group of men stepped out of the house and stood on the porch. "The hell you want!" one of the men on the porch yelled from across the yard.

"Where is Sonneillon? I need to speak to him!" Rosier answered.

One of the men stepped into the house to find Sonneillon. I shifted closer to the home to see Sonneillon sitting at a table surrounded by his subordinates, playing poker.

Sonniellon stepped outside and stood amongst the soldiers that were on the porch.

"What are you doing here, wench? Shouldn't you be at your post waiting for Lucifer?" Sonneillon barked at Rosier.

"Lucifer has already arrived! He's asked me to invite you to a celebration in honor of his arrival!"

"Shit!" Sonniellon hissed under his breath. His hands gripped the railing of the porch, cracking the wood.

"Well!" Sonneillon stood straight to reply, "Tell Lucifer I'm not going to his welcome party! Instead, you should tell him that I no longer serve him! Go and tell him that his reign is over!"

"Sonneillon!" Rosier called out. "You've betrayed your master and will suffer his wrath!"

Sonneillon walked down the steps of the porch. "What are you talking about, Rosier!" he asked loudly. "Did you think you could come here to kill me? I dare you to try it!"

Rosier stayed quiet. She sat on her horse, watching Sonneillon as he walked back to enter the house.

Then a rumbling sound emanated from the forest behind Rosier. The sound grew louder and louder. Finally, Sonneillon turned back to see an army of white-skinned creatures pouring out of the woods, charging toward Sonneillon.

The creatures moved quickly, and Sonneillon's soldiers tried to fire their guns at them, but the animals were too fast, tearing apart the soldiers as they poured out of the house. Sonneillon ran back into the place as the beasts jumped onto the roof of the house to kill the men guarding above.

Sonneillon ran through the house and exited out the back door to his horse and mounted it, making his escape into the forest. Rosier galloped quickly towards the woods, in pursuit of Sonneillon. Her army followed behind her. I mounted my horse and followed. Sonneillon was not too far ahead and after retreating into the woods and making his escape, Sonneillon reached a factory, just outside of the forest.

"Astaroth!" Sonneillon cried out. "I need your help, Astaroth!" He fell silent, and I heard a voice in my head that said,

"Who calls my name?"

WRATH

Raphael

I followed Gabriel to the room, which he claimed had no use. Gabriel then showed me the image of a man.

"Who's this?" I asked.

"His name is Aaron Weller. Aaron here is an ex-soldier, and he fought in the civil war. He is responsible for the death of eighteen me whom he killed in action during his military service. A friend of his gave him the nickname 'Tomahawk.'"

"So what of him?" I asked Gabriel.

"He's a warrior, Raphael. We need someone with his kind of ferocity."

"Are you sure we need someone like *him*?" I questioned.

"Yes. Lucifer is astute but won't expect us to resort to something like this. Besides, Raphael, this man just lost everything he valued most, and there is nothing more effective than a man with nothing to lose."

"I see. But how would this even work? Are you going to bring him here?" I asked.

"Well, yes. It's safe here, and our friend is now dead."

"He's dead?" I asked, confused. "What use is he to us then?"

"We can bring him back."

"You're going to revive him? You don't have that power."

"Well," Gabriel said awkwardly. "Not entirely. Of course, we can't just revive him. We'll let his spirit enter his body again, and he will operate under our direction."

"But he's dead," I muttered.

"Yes, but we can still use him. Trust me, Raphael."

I breathed deeply.

"All right," I said. "You're in charge either way."

"Thank you," Gabriel said.

"Okay, so, where is he?" I asked.

"I'm going to get him right now."

Aaron

"Whoa," I said out loud. "I'm probably gonna keep asking you this, but what is this place?"

"This is a library," Raphael explained. "This is where I keep the designs of all the weapons I've constructed."

The room was like a giant cabinet. The walls and the floor were of dark wood, like mahogany. The highest part of the walls was painted white, with light coming in through the glass ceiling. There were books and scrolls of paper scattered everywhere.

"Aaron," Raphael signaled me to approach the table where he was standing. I walked up some steps to the platform. A long table stood in the center next to a wall layered with windows.

"Aaron," Raphael said. "This is not what I wanted you to see. Come on."

Raphael walked past a wall of books that contained a staircase behind it. The steps led to a short hallway with glass cases displaying weapons. Raphael unlocked the door at the end of the hall and held it open.

"Who the hell are you people?" I asked in awe.

Raphael closed the door behind him and stood next to me to say,

"We're hunters."

The room was enormous, but what surprised me was how many weapons Raphael had stored. The room had tables and racks containing different blades and hand-held weaponry.

"Whoa," I said right after.

I walked through the room, admiring all of it.

"There's plenty to choose from, Aaron," Raphael informed.

"Yeah, but I don't know how to use any of these weapons," I stated.

"What is this?" I asked, taking a long rod from a wooden case on the wall.

"That is a Leviathan spear," Raphael stated.

"What does it do?"

Raphael looked back at me with a mischievous grin as he said, "It kills big things."

I took a moment to remember something. Then, I gave Raphael an answer he wasn't expecting.

"Can you get me to Virginia?"

"What's in Virginia?" Gabriel asked, appearing out of thin air. I didn't react this time.

"Can you get me there?" I continued.

Gabriel and Raphael exchanged looks before they agreed.

"Lead the way," Raphael said as he waved his hand to a doorway appearing out of thin air.

We all stepped out to a forest. Gabriel and Raphael followed me to a marked grave in the middle of the Virginia woods. I found the marker and walked forward past the grave. Gabriel walked up with Raphael, standing behind me. They didn't say anything.

I dug my hands into the dirt, tearing it apart, reaching deeper and deeper until my hands touched the case. I gripped the handle of the case and pulled it with all my strength. The case slid out from under the dirt. I reached out to take an item of clothing out of the case. I held up a blue coat with gold patches and put it on. Next, I took the first item and unwrapped the fabric around it.

A leather box containing my service pistol; sitting comfortably on fur. I placed the gun aside, reaching into the wooden case for the belt that holstered the pistol. I put it on, then I reached out to grab the last item in the case. I unwrapped the item and stared at the hatchet lying in my hand. I gripped the handle and felt something familiar.

Gabriel waved his hand, and the image of a different forest appeared before us.

"What's that?" I asked, loading the pistol.

"This is where you will find the enemy; hunt them and kill them all," Raphael said.

"Now?"

"Yes," Gabriel said, nodding his head, "We have to find Lucifer as quickly as possible."

I sighed heavily and stood up to look at Gabriel and Raphael.

"Okay," I said, "Let's do this."

Asmodeus

As I walked out of the woods, I could feel the atmosphere shift. The factory was just down the road—the place where I would find Astaroth. I strolled patiently, not rushing to what awaited me. Something in the air burned my skin violently, but the temperature was cold. I could feel pressure weighing down on me.

I stopped at the factory and turned to look back at the group of sacrifices I brought for Astaroth to consume.

I led the sacrifices into the factory and headed downstairs, where Astaroth lurked. I walked past the machinery into the darkness until I could no longer see the light until I could hear Astaroth.

I lit a torch and found Astaroth kneeling on the floor, covered by his black robes. I stepped into his chamber and stood behind him.

"Asmodeus," Astaroth muttered. He stood like the shadow of a monster, tall and broad with massive claws. He turned to face me and stepped into the light and his form changed. He was now in his human form. He looked at me with his hood over his head, covering half his face. "So, you came," He said, smiling.

"Astaroth," I replied.

Astaroth breathed heavily. "Do you know what I seek?" he asked.

"You want power; Lucifer sent me to help you."

"Then quit standing around and do as Lucifer commanded you."

"Okay," I muttered.

I pulled on the rope and forced the humans to kneel before Astaroth.

Astaroth took a different form and approached the sacrifices. His demonic form sunk his teeth into their necks to consume their spirit.

The bodies of each sacrifice made a loud thud as they plopped down in front of Astaroth, dead.

"Well," I said, wiping the blood from my sandal with a finger. "Step into the blood."

I took a step back and watched as Astaroth stepped into the boiling pool of blood on the floor. Once he was completely submerged, the blood began to turn black. The fluid became thick, like tar. Astaroth rose out of the pool of black tar, and it began covering his body as it bonded to his skin until he regained shape.

"Asmodeus raised his arms with fire in his hands, and the light illuminated more of the room, revealing the piles of corpses hidden in the shadows.

"Finally!" Astaroth said. "Now," He continued. "What are we going to do about Lucifer?"

"Astaroth!" A voice called out.

I looked at Astaroth as he walked past me. He was walking out towards the light, back into the realm of Earth. I followed behind him and could still hear the voice calling Astaroth's name. We were in the basement underneath the factory, where we met Sonneillon.

"Who calls my name?" Astaroth asked, revealing himself under the light.

"Master!" Sonneillon exclaimed as he knelt before Astaroth.

"What is it, Sonneillon?" Astaroth asked with an expression of disgust on his face.

"It's Rosier!" Sonneillon said dramatically. "She killed all my men and is coming here to kill me."

"She's coming here!" Sonneillon groveled like a hurt child.

Astaroth told Sonneillon to get off his knees and to stop embarrassing himself. Then, Astaroth walked past Sonneillon towards the staircase to go up. Sonneillon and I followed Astaroth until he stood outside the factory to see the edge of the forest where Rosier was waiting.

"Astaroth!" Rosier called out. "Where is Sonneillon?"

Astaroth didn't respond to what Rosier was saying. He removed his robe, revealing the black armor he was wearing. He then extended his arms to his sides and let out clouds of black smoke from his hands. The smoke began to form the twelve shadows, and the shadows became humanoid strangers, all dressed in armor, like Astaroth. The dark figures had long, black swords and hoods covering their heads. Astaroth drew his sword and pointed at Rosier, saying,

"You have no business here, Rosier! You've lifted your hand against one of your own, and I will kill you and use your blood to fuel my vengeance!"

Rosier said nothing back. She sat on her horse in silence, and then I could hear a rumbling sound coming from the trees, like a mountain raining down an avalanche. Something was coming, and just like an avalanche, a flood of white creatures poured out of the forest, charging toward Astaroth. Astaroth's army then attacked the army of white beasts. Rosier outnumbered Astaroth substantially, but that wasn't stopping him.

I watched as Astaroth's twelve shadows began tearing apart Rosier's creatures. The shadows moved swiftly, killing everything thrown at them. Rosier stayed back, watching as her army fell. Astaroth charged through the army of white, ripping the creatures to shreds and mowing them down with his massive sword.

Astaroth began to close in on Rosier, getting closer and closer, and just before Astaroth could get to her, Leonard appeared out of the trees and mounted Rosier's horse. Leonard fired his rifle, hitting Astaroth in the chest before pulling the straps on the horse, forcing it to gallop away into the forest.

I was in awe after watching Astaroth tear Rosier's army apart without taking a scratch, but I was more surprised by Leonard.

"Now, why would you go and something like that?" I said out loud. I looked at Sonneillon.

"You better hope Lucifer doesn't find out about this," I said to him.

Sonneillon looked at me and said,

"That's *your* job."

I scoffed before opening a portal and leaving the scene.

I had arrived back in Lucifer's chamber, where he sat upon his throne. Leonard stepped in after me. "My lord," Leonard said to Lucifer as he kneeled before him. "I have terrible news."

Leonard

I watched as Rosier and Astaroth engaged in an argument before deploying their armies into battle. Astaroth seemed to have the upper hand as he and his twelve shadows ripped apart Rosier's army. I noticed Asmodeus and Sonneillon were also watching from the factory. After Astaroth had finished defeating Rosier's army, he began charging toward her. I ran to Rosier to get out of there.

I could see the town standing past the forest. As we passed through the forest, we found the bodies of the demons scattered across the woods. We kept moving forward until We came across the body of Gressil. I stopped the horse and watched as Gressil knelt before us, breathing his dying breath.

"Is he still alive?" Rosier asked.

"No," I whispered before commanding Rosier's horse to keep moving until we had reached the town where Lucifer awaited.

Aaron

I turned away and stepped through the doorway. I could feel the dirt under my boots as I stepped onto the ground of the forest. I walked forward with my gun in my hand, unsure what I would find.

"Okay, Aaron," Gabriel's voice sounded in my head.

"What the?" I said in surprise. "How are you doing that?" I asked.

"Don't worry," Gabriel said.

"Okay," I said, "I'm guessing you're gonna tell me what to do also?"

"No. I will do that," Raphael's voice sounded in my head.

"What the hell?" I said, looking around."

"Aaron, focus," Raphael demanded. "You're going to find a group just ahead of you. Go where they are but don't get close."

"Alright," I said in agreement.

I walked forward until Gabriel told me to stop at a house surrounded by soldiers.

Nothing seemed to be happening. Then one stepped outside. The soldier was walking away into the woods.

"Hey, where are you going?" One of the guards standing on the roof of the house asked.

"I'm gonna take a piss!" the man shouted back.

"Okay, Aaron. He's going into the forest. Follow him," Raphael ordered.

"Right," I muttered.

I kept my distance from the man as he walked deeper into the woods. Finally, he stopped by a tree and started "doing his business."

"Aaron," Raphael said, "You need to interrogate him. Go."

"Got it," I whispered, taking my gun out. I moved as quietly as possible, keeping my eyes fixed on the soldier, but after pushing past a large tree, the soldier was gone.

I was in shock. My heart skipped a beat when I saw the soldier missing.

"Where did he go?" I asked.

"Go to where he was standing. But, be careful," Raphael said.

I did as Raphael had asked and walked over to where the man had been standing before. I looked around for any sign of where he could have gone but couldn't find anything.

"He's gone," I said. Raphael didn't say anything back.

I then could hear a distinct noise coming from somewhere near the tree. It sounded like breathing. I looked up slowly and saw a dark creature sitting on one of the tree branches. The creature smiled at me and quickly let itself fall from the tree. I tried to lift my gun to shoot it, letting out a gunshot, but the creature grabbed me by my coat and lifted me into the air as it flew up. The beast dropped me onto the ground, and I hit my head. The leaves crunched as my body hit the ground. The creature landed above me and placed its heavy foot on my chest.

"Well, what do we have here," the creature spoke hoarsely. A smile crept across its face. "You're not supposed to be here," it said. "We killed all the humans in this area. Who are you?"

I didn't say anything.

The creature scoffed and grinned. It had a very scary-looking appearance. Its skin was black as charcoal, and the irises in its eyes were yellow with pupils like little black beads. The creature smiled with its rotting, yellow teeth, spreading its giant, bat-like wings.

"I should eat you. I bet you taste delicious," the creature said, dragging a long, black claw against my cheek.

"I wouldn't do that. I carry diseases," I said blatantly.

The demon moved its foot to my head, and I groaned as it pressed down.

"You know," the demon said. "That shot was quite loud. I'm betting my subordinates are on their way here now. They'll come down here, and we'll have fun tearing you to pieces."

"Oh, yeah?" I asked, breathing heavily. "Why don't you just do it yourself?"

The demon shifted its foot, angrily reaching its hand back, ready to claw off my face. I closed my eyes and looked away, bracing myself, but nothing happened.

"What?" the demon asked, surprised as I was.

I opened my eyes to see Raphael standing over me, holding the demon's hand. Raphael then kicked the monster, sending it flying back against a tree. The demon smashed through the tree, splitting it in half.

"Aaron," Raphael said, "get out of here."

I got up off the ground and stepped behind Raphael. He extended his hand, and my pistol flew up from the ground into his palm before he handed it to me.

Raphael stepped forward, and I could see the demon rising to its feet. Raphael stood firm, waiting. The monster looked at Raphael before charging ahead and flying towards us. Raphael didn't move. A set of eagle's wings appeared on Raphael's back before he charged forward towards the demon until they collided and flew up into the sky. I looked back and heard someone approaching.

"Aaron," Gabriel's voice appeared in my mind, telling me to run.

I began to run into the forest until I thought I was safe. I stopped to lean against a tree and placed my hands against my knees, breathing heavily. I looked up when I heard the sound of branches cracking loudly, then a loud thud. It sounded like something had fallen. I moved over to investigate. Taking the gun out of the holster, I followed the trail of broken branches until I found Raphael standing over the body of the creature that had attacked me. I uncocked the gun and put it back in the holster as I walked over to Raphael.

"Raphael?" I asked. "Are you okay?" Raphael wasn't saying anything. He was just staring at the dead demon.

"Raphael?"

Raphael finally turned to look at something that was approaching us. "We have to go," he said as he opened a doorway. I followed him in, and we were gone.

Raphael and I had arrived at The Spirit House. Gabriel was waiting for us at the end of the hallway.

"We have a problem," Gabriel said, looking at Raphael.

"I know," Raphael said.

I walked in after Raphael as Gabriel held the door open. I walked over to sit at the table.

"So, what happened? What was that?" I asked, breaking the silence.

"It was a sentry," Gabriel said firmly.

"What is that?" I asked with uncertainty.

"They're Lucifer's watchers," Raphael answered, "They tell him everything."

I turned back to look at Raphael standing behind me.

"Aaron, we can't let them tell Lucifer that you were there," Gabriel said in a steady tone, "They can't know that you're alive."

I looked at the floor.

"What do you want me to do?" I asked nervously.

"What we brought you here to do," Raphael responded, "Kill them all."

I looked at Raphael again. His eyes locked on me. He wasn't playing around, so I couldn't afford to either. I stood up and told them to send me back in. Gabriel nodded and stepped away from me to open a doorway back into the forest, and I walked in.

My boots squished against the dirt as I stepped out of the doorway, moving forward, taking my gun out of its holster. The leaves crunched as I stepped against the ground, walking up a short hill, uncertain of what I would find at the top because I couldn't see. I finally reached the top, and just as I was going to call out to Gabriel to inform him that the area seemed clear, a man stepped out from behind a tree.

The man froze when he saw me. I saw a rifle in his hands, but the barrel pointed toward the ground. We looked at each other for a moment, and then I moved my pistol up to shoot him, but he quickly tackled me down and we tumbled down the hill. I quickly looked for my gun, then heard the man approaching me, so I took the ax from my belt to cut him down, but the man hit me with the butt of his rifle before I could land the swing. I fell backward and went dizzy for a moment.

The man knelt over me and put the barrel of his rifle against my neck. I saw my pistol lying beside me when he pushed my head down. I reached for it and grasped the handle.

"Time to die, worm," the man said, cocking back the hammer of his gun, but just before he could fire, I moved the barrel away from my neck, placed the barrel of my pistol against his collar, and pulled the trigger. I expected blood but instead, a black liquid poured out of him, spraying my face.

I pushed the man off and knelt over him, taking my ax straight to his face, screaming as I did it. Then, finally, I breathed heavily and stood up, taking my ax and walking away.

I walked forward and could hear the sounds of men talking amongst themselves.

"What was that?" one asked in a loud voice.

"I don't know!" another voice responded.

"Well, find out!" another exclaimed.

I stopped and waited behind a tree.

"There's more of them," Raphael's voice sounded. "Just ahead."

I could hear someone approaching, and once they were close enough, I jumped out from behind the tree and lodged my ax into their throat. A man, just like the one from before, but blood like oil spilling out from his neck.

"Demons," Raphael said with contempt.

I kicked the demon back and noticed another one of them standing behind him. I aimed my pistol and fired just before he could move his rifle up to shoot. The bullet punctured the demon's head, killing it instantly. The body dropped and let out a loud thud as it fell. I took cover behind a tree to reload the used bullets and heard another one of them approaching.

I took the ax and threw it, but the demon was hit by the handle and not the blade. The ax clunked loudly as the wood hit the demon's head. I quickly moved toward the monster as it tried to regain its balance, and I kicked it to the floor to shove my gun in its face and shoot it. I saw two more making their way toward me and aimed my pistol from behind a tree at the one that was closest and fired. The bullet penetrated the demon's head and hit the soldier further away, killing them both.

It seemed there weren't any more of them left, just a small group of them moving together toward me. I peeked behind one of the trees and aimed my gun at them. There were three of them, but I tensed up when I recognized one of them.

"Marvin," I whispered. "He's here."

"Aaron," Gabriel spoke, "If you have a shot, take it. Now."

I cocked back the gun's hammer, shaking with anger as I did, and let out two shots, killing the two demons with Gressil. He froze as I stepped out from behind the tree.

"Well, this is a surprise," Gressil said.

He seemed to know who I was. I didn't respond, keeping my gun pointed at him. Marvin held his shotgun in his hands, but it seemed I got the drop on him. Gressil opened his mouth to say something, but I wasn't going to listen.

"So, you gonna just-" as Marvin was going to speak, he was interrupted by a bullet hitting his chest. Black fluid gushed out of him, and he looked down to see the wound before dropping to his knees.

I lowered my gun as he began to die slowly. I placed my gun in its holster and walked away from him. I told Gabriel to open a doorway so I could leave the forest.

Gabriel welcomed me as I walked out of the doorway into the spirit house.

He and Raphael were standing in the hallway, waiting for me.

"How do you feel?" Raphael asked.

I thought about it, but I didn't know what to say.

"I feel fine," I muttered.

Raphael seemed doubtful by the expression he had made. He didn't say anything as we began walking to the library.

"So," I said as we walked in, "Who's next?"

Gabriel walked up, saying, "We're finally making progress. Hopefully, we can find the others quickly."

SONNEILLON

Asmodeus

"My lord," Leonard said, stepping into the chamber. "I have terrible news."

"What is it?" Lucifer asked.

"It's Gressil, my lord. He's dead." Leonard answered, kneeling before Lucifer.

I was surprised. I was expecting Leonard to say something different.

"How do you know this?" Lucifer asked. His expression was unchanged.

"We found him in the woods. He was still breathing, but he was already dead."

"Who found him? You and whom?" Lucifer asked.

"Rosier, my lord."

Lucifer sat up. "Take me to him," he said.

"As you command." Leonard stood up and started walking away.

"Leonard," Lucifer said, stopping him.

Leonard turned to Lucifer.

"Where is Rosier?" Lucifer asked.

"She's upstairs," Leonard said and turned away as he kept walking.

Lucifer didn't say anything as he stormed out angrily. I looked at Lucifer's throne and stepped before it, taking a moment to look around and realizing I was alone. I sat down slowly, letting the black smoke that rose from the throne enter my veins, turning them black. I began to contort and twist, gritting my teeth and absorbing the throne's power, but it was too much. I slid off the throne and fell to the floor. My veins returned to their normal state, and I could barely move from the power I had just absorbed. I then forced myself to stand on my feet, placed my hand on my head, and began laughing. I knew if Lucifer had seen what I had done, he would make me pay. but I wanted more.

I transported myself to where Lucifer had gone and found Leonard, Lucifer, and Rosier standing before Gressil's corpse in the woods.

"What happened here?" Lucifer asked. Everyone around him stood silent. Finally, Lucifer stepped closer to Gressil and extended his hand toward him.

"Fine," Lucifer said. "I'll see for myself." Black smoke emanated from Gressil's mouth and into Lucifer's hand. The smoke entered Lucifer's veins, and he closed his eyes as he absorbed it.

"Well," Lucifer whispered with a smile. "You tricky little devils."

Lucifer turned to the group behind him. "It's time we took our next step. Gather the captains and my legions."

"What are you going to do?" Leonard asked.

"I'm going to show them what we can do."

Lucifer walked past the group and disappeared into a portal, leaving us.

"What do you think he saw?" Rosier asked.

"I don't know," Leonard muttered, "but it doesn't sound good."

Leonard walked away towards the town.

"Where are you going?" Rosier asked.

Leonard didn't turn back as he walked away, answering, "I'm gonna get a drink!"

I stood quiet and kept looking at Gressil's rotting corpse as it began to smell, letting out a foul stench like rotting meat and eggs.

"What now?" Rosier asked, interrupting my gaze.

I turned to Rosier, answering her question. "We wait," I said. "I need to see what Lucifer is going to do." I walked away and opened a portal back to Lucifer, but I turned back before the portal had closed to see Rosier kneel next to Gressil, closing his eyes before returning to the town.

Leonard

"Another one," I said. The barkeep slid the bottle over to my hand. I heard Rosier step into the bar and sit next to me, but we were not alone, as a small group of other demons was seated at one of the tables.

"How are you?" Rosier asked as she sat down.

"I'm fine," I said as I poured the whiskey into the glass.

"You look stressed. Lucifer has you doing a lot of work."

"Lucifer has me doing what he needs me to do. I don't question my service to him." I took another long sip of the glass before pouring more.

"And what if I told you that you deserve more than to be serving Lucifer," Rosier said.

I took a sip from the glass and cocked an eyebrow. "I don't deserve more," I muttered before taking another gulp.

"I just think we all deserve more than what Lucifer is giving us," Rosier stated, placing her hand on my thigh.

I moved Rosier's hand away, saying, "In another life, I would have agreed with you, but I owe Lucifer my life and service as he is the only reason I am even here, you, too." I turned to Rosier with an expression of anger.

Rosier stayed quiet. I then stood up, put on my coat to leave, and tipped my hat to Asmodeus, who was stepping into the bar as I walked out. I stood outside for a moment to listen.

Asmodeus walked towards Rosier and stood behind her. "Rosier," Asmodeus said, "Lucifer wants to see you."

The group of demons who were sitting at the table all stood up and surrounded Rosier. Rosier finished the drink that I had left behind and stood up to face Asmodeus. Rosier didn't say anything and complied with Asmodeus. She then stepped into the portal that Asmodeus had opened for her, and Asmodeus followed.

Lucifer

A portal appeared before me. Asmodeus and Rosier stepped into my chamber.

"Rosier," I said with a welcoming tone.

Rosier walked up to the altar and kneeled before me.

"You called for me, master?" Rosier asked.

I stayed quiet, and the short silence was interrupted by Rosier as she let out a painful wail. A shadow had pierced her chest, and she began to bleed on the floor. I sat forward and watched as rosier cried out in pain.

"You know," I spoke up, "Asmodeus claims that you went to Astaroth without my knowledge, and you attacked him!"

"He's betraying you!" Rosier let out painfully.

"Is that so?" I asked. "Astaroth told me something similar. He said you were not to be trusted, and I should hand you over to him so he can tear you apart!"

Rosier groaned painfully as she tried to force herself to stand. The shadow had gone away and Rosier's blood began to spill even more. She held her hand over the wound, trying to suppress the flow of blood. I stood up from my throne before sitting on the steps of the altar and held Rosier's head on my lap and caressed her hair.

"What am I going to do with all of you?" I asked, letting out a deep sigh.

Rosier looked up at me with tears, saying, "I'm sorry. I was protecting you."

I wiped the tears away as Rosier's wounds began to heal.

"I don't need you to protect me," I said softly. "But I also can't have you dishonoring my name."

I threw Rosier away aggressively, knocking her down to the floor before I sat back down on my throne. There was a moment of silence, but it was interrupted by a demon who had stepped into the chamber. The soldier walked towards us and kneeled, saying,

"My lord, Sonneillon is outside. He is requesting your appearance."

I sighed with frustration and stood up again, but stopped when I felt a sharp pain and a loud ringing in my head. Asmodeus moved over to me, asking,

"Lucifer, are you all right?"

I took a deep breath, stepped down from the altar, and told the demon to go with me to meet with Sonneillon. Asmodeus stayed behind with Rosier.

I stepped out of the portal that led to the street outside. Sonneillon stood in the distance, pacing back and forth, angrily calling out to me.

"Lucifer!" Sonneillon called out when he saw me. "Bring me that whore so I can tear her flesh apart!"

I stood in silence, watching Sonneillon pace back and forth angrily. Sonneillon had with him a black horse whose eyes were completely black with demon blood dripping from its mouth.

"What do you want, Sonneillon?" I asked.

Sonneillon stopped pacing and screamed, "I want Rosier!"

These animals were pushing me to my limit. Before I remembered, I had none.

"Bring her to me, now!" Sonneillon screamed with anger, but Sonneillon quickly stopped as I began to drain the life force out of Sonneillon from where he was standing.

"Now, you listen to me, boy!" I screamed, "I don't have to do anything you tell me! If I wanted to, I could drain your life force until you're nothing but a rotting puddle of demonic filth! So, I suggest you speak to me with respect before I show you what pain is!" my power made Sonneillon cry out in pain as he rolled around on the ground.

I lifted my hand and opened a portal to my chamber. A soldier pushed Rosier out of the doorway, and she fell to the ground.

"Is this what you want?" I asked.

Sonneillon stood up and looked at me, but not a word exited his mouth. I pulled on Rosier's hair, showing her face to Sonneillon. "I will hand her over, and you can do whatever you desire, but I never want to see your face again, Sonneillon! Not after demonstrating such disrespect! Consider this mercy."

Sonneillon stayed quiet as I handed Rosier over to him. Rosier looked up at Sonneillon in silence. Sonneillon struck Rosier in the face, knocking her unconscious. He then carried Rosier up and mounted her on his horse before riding into the woods.

Aaron

"Aaron," Gabriel said, stepping into the room. "I've found our next target."

I stood up from the chair and said, "Show me."

Gabriel led me to the room where Raphael had shown me how the enemy looked. He stepped into the center of the room, and I followed and stood next to him as an image appeared before us.

"It's Sonneillon. I tracked him already; He's in a barn outside Black Rose. It was quite simple. These demons have kept themselves close to Lucifer. I thought they would have expanded by now, but I guess not."

"Right. Well, send me in. I'll take care of Sonneillon."

Gabriel nodded, and the image faded away.

"Be careful, Aaron." Raphael's voice echoed across the room. I saw Raphael standing at the door with his arms crossed, as he always does. "This demon is not as powerful as the others," Raphael continued. "But he is violent and dangerous, and the only way to stop him is to kill him."

"That's what I plan to do," I stated.

Raphael didn't say anything, but he gave me a nod.

"Aaron," Gabriel interrupted. "We're very close. After this, I hope to reach Lucifer finally, and we can end this."

I nodded in agreement. "Okay," I said. "Let's go get this bastard."

Gabriel nodded and opened a doorway for me to step in. I appeared in a grassy field with the moon shining above. I walked forward as Gabriel and Raphael guided me to where I needed to go. After a while, I finally reached a small barn next to a house that looked like it had been torn apart by a demolition crew. I could see it under the light of a fire in front of the barn. A group of men dragged a woman out of the barn, pushing and kicking her to the ground.

"That's Sonneillon," Raphael stated.

"I see him," I whispered.

Sonneillon was dragging the woman by her hair. I then saw two men carrying a large wooden next to the fire. They laid the cross on the ground and placed the woman on top. I could hear them hammering nails into her hands, causing her to wail in pain. The hammers kept pounding until they switched to her other hand and kept going.

Once the hammering had stopped, I saw two men pulling on ropes attached to the cross. Unfortunately, one of the ropes had ripped, and the cross fell to the ground. The woman cried out in pain as the wood pounded against the dirt.

"Dammit!" One of the men exclaimed. "I told you to get a thicker rope!"

Whoever he was yelling at didn't reply. Instead, Sonneillon stepped back, away from the fire as two men re-tied the rope around the cross and were finally able to raise it over the fire.

"Witness!" Sonneillon exclaimed. "Witness my fury!"

The fire began to creep up the cross, engulfing it in flames. The woman's dress began to burn as the fire climbed higher and higher until it finally started to consume her. The woman cried out as the flames seared her skin.

"These guys are animals," I muttered.

"Focus, Aaron," Raphael's voice sounded, "They don't know you're here. Take them out quickly and get out."

"Understood."

"This is my fury," Sonneillon screamed. "This is my revenge!"

My gun firing quickly snuffed out Sonneillon's voice as the bullet hit his leg. Sonniellon yelped in pain, and the men around him turned to me but were quickly extinguished by my bullets hitting each of their heads. I walked towards Sonneillon and shot one of the demons lying on the ground, finishing them.

I dragged Sonneillon by his hair as he kicked and screamed. I didn't listen to what he was saying, then I threw him into the fire and fired two shots into his back as he tried to run away, covered in flames.

Then all I could hear was the flickering of the fire. Then I heard a voice speaking to me, saying, "What are you?." The voice sounded hoarse and croaky.

I looked up to see the woman was still alive.

"I watched you die," The woman continued. "I....know you."

I didn't know what to say.

"I'm sorry," I said to her as I cocked back the hammer of my gun to shoot her. I pulled the trigger, but the gun clicked empty.

The woman made an expression that appeared to be a grin, saying, "I am not at your mercy."

I lowered my gun and asked, "You tried to warn me?"

The woman forced herself to say, "Yes."

"You could've stopped them?" I asked, putting my gun away.

"No," The woman replied, "All I could do was tell you."

I looked at her and said, "Then do us both a favor. Burn."

I turned and walked away, letting the fire rage on, consuming Rosier and Sonneillon.

Leonard

Asmodeus and I stood outside the barn, watching as Lucifer arrived, surrounded by a posse of his subordinates.

"This is starting to get complicated," Lucifer stated. He looked at the burned body of Rosier as it hung from the cross, smoke still rising from the charred wood.

"What are we going to do?" Asmodeus asked.

Lucifer removed the hood covering his head and turned back to look at Asmodeus. "I want that dead man's head on a stick!"

"Who, my lord?" Asmodeus asked with a confused tone.

Lucifer grinned, asking, "You have no idea, do you?"

Asmodeus looked even more confused. "Who are you referring to?" he asked.

"You and Leonard made a mistake, Asmodeus," Lucifer said, making his smile bigger. "We're being hunted down by a fucking human." Lucifer sounded angrier as he forced the words out.

I moved closer to Lucifer, asking, "You don't mean-?"

"Aaron Weller," Lucifer stated, interrupting me.

Lucifer turned away from the group and began walking back toward the town.

Everyone followed him there. I looked at Rosier's burned body. There was something in me, like sadness, but also regret. I stayed quiet, not saying a word.

Lucifer then told me to gather his remaining forces in Black Rose.

Lucifer sat on the church's steps, waiting for everyone to gather so they could hear what he had to say. The group of demons surrounding him grew larger until all of them were standing outside. The demons all bowed and rose to their feet, waiting for Lucifer to speak.

"My dear servants!" Lucifer said, rising to his feet. "I believe it is time to let you all know that we are currently being hunted down by a group of our divine brethren, as we should have expected. Three of my captains have turned up dead!

I gathered you here because I need all of you to prepare yourselves for what is coming. Trust no one and kill all who threaten our purpose. We will bring upon the destruction of this world, and rule over it like kings. No longer will we be hiding in the shadow of humanity! We will conquer this place and destroy all who oppose us!"

The crowd cheered with ferocity, and as the crowd roared with excitement, Lucifer pulled me to the side and told me to assemble an army to go out and burn down all the nearby towns and exterminate the population.

I obeyed Lucifer's order and rounded up a group of soldiers. Lucifer called Asmodeus, and they both headed back to his chamber.

HUNTERS

Gabriel

"Aaron," I called out, appearing before him in the library. Aaron leaned against the wooden railing of the floor above. "What is it?" he asked.

"Come with me."

I held the door open, waiting for Aaron to come downstairs. Instead, he rushed down the staircase steps and walked out the door, putting his coat on.

"Where are we going?" Aaron asked.

"Where's Raphael?" I asked, ignoring his question.

"I don't know," Aaron muttered. "He walked out of the library like twenty minutes ago."

"Raphael," I called out.

"What is it?" Raphael asked.

"Meet me in The watch room. There's been a development. Lucifer has come out of hiding."

"What's going on?" Raphael asked.

"Lucifer has lost mind," I stated.

"Where is he?"

"The town's center. He's assembling his forces."

Raphael appeared in the watcher's room. "So, we know where Lucifer is?" Raphael asked, approaching Aaron and me.

"He's revealing his position. This might be our only chance to finish this quickly," I stated and looked at Aaron.

"No," Raphael said. "He can't go in by himself. There will be too many of them."

"We just need him to get to Lucifer," I stated. "He won't see Aaron coming."

Aaron stepped forward, standing confidently. "Raphael," he said, "I can do this. It's what you guys brought me here to do, right?"

Raphael sighed, "fine," he said. "But don't engage him, just get close, and we'll handle the rest."

Aaron

"Aaron," Raphael spoke as I stepped out of the doorway.

"I'm here," I said.

"Are you ready to do this?" Raphael asked.

"Yeah," I said. "Let's finish this."

I stepped forward, taking my gun from its holster. I gripped the handle tightly. These woods extended very far, so I knew it would take some time, but I was ready.

"Aaron, they're not far ahead. So keep moving," Raphael said.

"Okay," I replied.

Just as Raphael had said, I could spot a group of demons moving in the distance through the trees. They were on my right, so I had an excellent chance to flank them.

"Aaron," Raphael said. "Do not engage. Two more groups are moving behind them. Find Lucifer."

Raphael was quiet for a moment. "Okay," he said, "Gabriel is going to distract them. Get ready to move."

I noticed a figure moving through the woods, close to where the group of demons was moving. A figure dressed in white appeared before them. I looked closer and watched as the demons panicked. I could hear them calling out to the stranger, saying,

"Hey! What are you doing here?"

There seemed to be no reply from the stranger. Instead, the figure stood before them. I looked around to see if I could spot any more demons coming this way before turning back to the stranger and watching them run away. Raphael told me to move.

"Get down," Raphael ordered.

I moved closer to them, concealing myself behind a tree.

"What's going on?" I asked.

"Something's coming," Raphael said.

I began to hear a sound coming from the trees. The air grew colder, and I tensed up as An army marched toward me. The galloping sound of their horses sounded like war drums, but I was looking at the front man. He wore a black hat and a black blazer. I could hear the jingling of the silver spurs of his black boots. It was him,

"Leonard."

"Standby, Aaron," Raphael instructed. "Let's wait and see what they do."

The army stopped moving, and they were standing in silence. The wind howled as it moved through the trees. I knew what was about to happen. That is the last thing you hear on the battlefield before someone dies.

"What are they doing?" Raphael asked.

"They're just...standing there."

I tried to look closely at what was happening as the army of demons stayed quiet. Then the leaves rustled as something was coming from the other side of the forest, moving towards the demon army. The sound grew louder and louder until I could finally see what was happening. More demons appeared out of the woods but were not on the side where Leonard was standing.

"Now, what the hell is this?" Leonard asked.

No one answered. Everyone stayed quiet until a voice answered, saying, "Now, Leonard, let's not be hasty."

Leonard seemed confused as he tried to see who had answered his question. And from amongst the group of demons, a man appeared, walking towards Leonard.

"Who's that guy?" I asked.

"Astaroth," Raphael answered.

"Aaron, you're going to have to move through them. Get to Lucifer."

"Okay," I said. "Should I just let the demons kill each other?"

"Yes, avoid fighting them."

"Alright."

I kept watching, waiting to see what would happen. Astaroth and Leonard were still talking. They kept talking until Leonard drew his weapon and fired at Astaroth. The demons on Leonard's side charged forward and engaged Astaroth's troops.

I stood up and watched. Raphael's voice interrupted my gaze, telling me to run, and I moved through the battlefield, swiftly moving past the demons as they began to fight. The sound of guns boomed loudly, and I could hear the scream as they died in front of me. I quickly jogged past the fighting, thinking I was safe, but I was quickly stopped by the hand of Lucifer wrapping itself around my neck and holding me up in the air.

"You know," Lucifer's voice sounded as he appeared before me. "You're starting to get really annoying."

I tried moving, but the grip of his hand was choking the life out of me. I could hear Raphael's voice fading away until there was only silence, and I could only see darkness.

Raphael

"Aaron!...Aaron!" I called out. He seemed to have been left unconscious. Aaron was no longer responding to me.

"What happened?" Gabriel asked, appearing before me.

"I lost Aaron."

"Where did he go?"

"Lucifer took him," I stated.

"Then we're going in."

I nodded, and we stepped out of the room. We walked down the hallway as our wardrobe changed, walking into the doorway that had opened before us. I could see the forest and the trees waiting.

The wind blew quietly, softly stirring the leaves on the ground. I held onto my sword as we moved forward, on our way to save Aaron. I could hear the sound of the demons fighting amongst themselves. Gabriel and I approached until we found a group of soldiers standing guard. They all stood around, watching us.

"Well, how about that? These boys brought knives to a gunfight!" One of the demons exclaimed. "Let's show them why they need to get with the times."

I looked at Gabriel and said, "All of them."

Gabriel nodded.

The demon soldier aimed his rifle, but just before he could fire, I stood in front of him with my sword in his throat. The demon choked on his blood as it filled his esophagus. The other monsters were dumbfounded by what had just happened. They fumbled with their weapons, still shocked by what they had just seen. Then, before they could even attack, Gabriel quickly took them down as he multiplied himself, diving into five. Each version rushed to kill the other demon soldiers before the divisions disappeared, and only Gabriel remained.

I extended my hand, and a black lion appeared next to me with a hawk mounted on my shoulder. I pointed to the battlefield and unleashed the beasts on the demons. Then, Gabriel and I moved forward into the chaos.

I stood in the woods, surrounded by demon corpses, I was going to call out to Gabriel since we had split up, but a voice spoke to me, appearing behind me.

"Well, this is interesting," the voice stated. I looked back and found Astaroth standing behind me; he stepped out from behind a tree and revealed himself, along with his twelve shadows. I looked at him but didn't say anything.

"What's the matter?" he asked. "You don't like being outnumbered?"

I lifted my sword, preparing to attack as I said, "No, you're outnumbered."

Astaroth scoffed, "Die."

Astaroth lunged forward with his massive sword in his hand. I jumped over him as he passed under me, a giant, black bow appeared in my hand, and I quickly fired a volley of arrows at Astaroth's shadows and slew each one of them with ease until they were nothing but dust and smoke. It happened so quickly that Astaroth stood in silence. Two of my arrows had pierced his back. He seemed shocked but quickly became angry and lunged forward to strike me. Gabriel appeared behind Astaroth with his blade sticking out of Astaroth's chest, slowly pulling out the sword from Astaroth's back. Astaroth fell silent before collapsing to the ground.

Gabriel and I had eradicated all of Lucifer's forces. Gabriel and I were the only ones standing. The town of Black Rose was silent. The rotting corpses of the demonic soldiers stunk up the air. We were making our way to the chamber. Gabriel stood in the center of the town square.

"This is it," Gabriel said. He turned to look at the chapel behind him. "The seal we placed on Aaron is leading me inside the church. Lucifer's corridors are in there."

"Let's go get Aaron and finish this."

We entered the chapel into the empty hall with only the sound of our footsteps. Gabriel and I stopped at the podium at the end of the hall.

"Hm," I said, "This is interesting."

I looked closer to see a black spot floating in the air, almost invisible.

"Negative matter," I stated.

"That's the entrance," Gabriel replied.

I looked at Gabriel. He nodded, assuring that he was ready. He opened the portal, sustaining the negative energy that burst out from it. The portal formed the black doorway, and we stepped in, appearing in a long, black corridor.

"Here we go," I said, taking my sword. Gabriel walked alongside me through the long hallways.

"It's up ahead," Gabriel informed.

"Keep your eyes open," I said, "Could be more of them down here."

Gabriel nodded right before we heard a sound down the hall. I looked at Gabriel, and we moved to see what made the noise. We stopped at a room in one of the corridors. The door had been left open. Something was moving around inside.

"Suprise them," I said to Gabriel. He understood and turned invisible.

I stepped into the room and looked for the cause of the noise. I turned to find a man fumbling around with objects at a table on the other side of the room. He hadn't noticed me yet.

"Who are you?" I said to the man. He was startled by my appearance as he quickly turned to look at me.

"Uh, Hello," The man said. "You know you shouldn't pop up on people like that. You have to announce yourself."

I stared at him. He must have been joking.

"Who are you?" I asked again, raising my sword.

The man chuckled loudly, then stopped.

"Whoops," The man said. His head turned up as Gabriel appeared next to him, holding a blade to his neck.

"Speak your name," Gabriel commanded.

"My name is Balberith," The man answered.

"Balberith the blasphemer," I said, approaching him. "I haven't heard that name in a while."

"Do I know you, fellas?" Balberith asked.

Gabriel and I did not answer. Then, a loud crash sounded from across the room. I turned to see what happened, Gabriel turned his attention to the noise, and I looked back at Balberith as he opened a portal and walked back into it. Gabriel turned and tried to grab Balberith, but he slipped away. Gabriel's hand moved through the portal as it turned into black smoke.

Gabriel looked at me and shook his head. I turned back to where the sound came from; a dark object stood in the corner of the room, A tall structure covered by a black cloth. I removed the fabric to find a cage made to fit a human, and in the corner sat a little boy.

"Is that a human child?" Gabriel asked.

"Yeah," I replied, approaching the cage.

The boy's back was turned. He reached out, took a dented metal dish sitting next to him, and shot it at the wall. The plate bounced back next to him, more dented than before. Pieces of the wall crumbled away, damaged by the metal dish.

"Who brought you here?" I asked the boy as he reached for the dish, but his hand stopped.

The boy stood up and turned to face Gabriel and me. The boy approached and stood before me. I kneeled to look at him. The boy didn't reply. He simply stood there, quietly staring. The child then reached his hand out quickly to scratch me. Claws extended out from his fingers, but he didn't touch me as my energy field prevented him from doing so. The boy pushed against the energy until it burned him, and he stepped away. The boy rubbed his hand and sat in the corner again.

"What did they do to him?" Gabriel asked. It was concerning to see something like this. This was crossing a line. "We have to take him to The Spirit. He'll know what to do," Gabriel concluded.

"I agree," I said. I extended my hand in the boy's direction, making him sleep. Gabriel stepped into the cage and lifted the boy against his shoulder.

"I'll take him there. " Go find Aaron," Gabriel instructed as a portal appeared next to him. I gave Gabriel a nod, and he left.

THE DARK

Aaron

I woke up in a dark room. The cold, hard floor stung my face. I looked around to see only darkness. My hands reddened as I forced myself to see where I was, but I could barely see anything as a bright light shined down. I looked around and scanned the area, but I couldn't tell what this place was. Then I turned when I heard a voice that said,

"Well, look who finally woke up. Welcome."

I turned to see Lucifer sitting at the top of the steps where I was lying. Asmodeus was standing across the room in the dark.

"You," I hissed at Asmodeus.

"What is this place?" I asked.

Lucifer sat silently for a brief moment before answering, "This is where I was born."

I didn't know what to say to that. So I stepped forward and approached him. As I did, Asmodeus reached for the knife in his robe, but Lucifer signaled him to stop.

"You've become quite a problem for me, Aaron," Lucifer said in a soft but menacing tone.

I stayed put, watching Lucifer as I said, "Why did you bring me here?"

Lucifer grinned and answered, "You are not the only one who has lost something, Aaron. I once sat upon a chair of pure gold, decorated with the rarest materials in the universe. I touched the sun and caressed the stars. I was a child of the Almighty. I was his brightest star. Born in heaven, but I fell. I was cast out of my home.

But, I knew I didn't deserve to go alone, so I took as many with me as possible. So, I do know how it feels to lose everything," Lucifer concluded.

I didn't say anything. The room was quiet. The air became colder. I kept my gaze fixed on Lucifer.

I lifted my head slightly and said, "I just wanted to be left alone with my wife and die in peace."

Lucifer's expression became more serious as he sat down on his throne. "I could never understand something like that," he said.

"No. You never will...." I stated.

We fell silent. Lucifer lifted his hand in the air. I was confused by his gesture, but suddenly, I felt pain. Horrible, searing pain. I fell to the floor, letting out wails of suffering. I looked up at Lucifer, hatred in my eyes. I only looked at certain things this way, which I felt I needed to destroy.

"What are you?" I asked.

Lucifer sat quietly before lowering his hand and said, "Let me show you."

I felt my head pulsating. Then, a sharp pain began to grow, creeping from my ears to my brain. My vision was turning black, and I felt like I was suffocating. I tried to move, but I was in incredible pain. My body quivered, and I became cold as ice.

"Stare into the abyss," Lucifer whispered.

I couldn't fight whatever Lucifer was doing to me. I gave up. Gave in. I was in darkness. I had blacked out.

Darkness surrounded me again. I felt nothing around me, not even the ground under my feet. A light appeared above, blinding me. I was being lowered onto the dark floor, the light revealing the space around me. Lights began to flash through the darkness that surrounded me. The light above shut off as the red flashes became more intense. A deep growl echoed through the dark as I walked forward to see a wall appear in front of me. More lights appeared behind the wall, through the translucent surface.

The sound of something pounding as the lights flashed synchronized with a massive heart beating. The red flashes behaved like nerves.

The ground shook, and the massive wall began to split in half, opening up. I stepped in between the walls. Red lights flashed around me as I walked deeper between the gigantic structures. Only darkness awaited me. I walked until the lights faded out, and it was pitch black. Then, a light appeared in the air again. The light shined down onto a tall shape in front of me, then more lights appeared, revealing what stood in front of me.

The room was bright, and I could see the form of a tall being trapped in a dark matter that covered the being's body; a human body but a thousand times as big with a black, metal mask that adorned the head of the creature, covering its eyes and a set of, massive, mangled, black wings that suspended the beast in the air. The black matter floated around the enormous being, a black goo coming from out of the darkness, outside of the light, and the red energy that flowed through the black matter, red energy that flowed through the tall being. I didn't know what I was looking at and felt a fear I hadn't felt in a long time.

Virginia, 1861

That morning sky, I remembered it—nothing like sitting in the cold, wet forest, waiting to ambush a bunch of rebels. I looked over to the young private sitting in front of me. He seemed nervous and too young to be in the military, and he was.

"You alright, kid?" I asked the young man. It seemed he didn't hear since there was no reaction, so I kicked his leg to get his attention. The young man looked up and blinked rapidly. He wasn't sure why I had kicked him.

"What's your name, kid?" I asked.

"My name is Bill," the private replied.

"That's it? Just Bill?"

Bill looked away.

"I can't read my last name."

"Because it's not your name, Right?" I said, handing him a cigarette.

Bill took the cigarette, and I lit it for him.

"You shouldn't be in a place like this," I said.

Bill puffed the cigarette and threw it away, saying,

"I ain't got no other place to go."

"Well, you oughta know," I said, "I've done this plenty of times. I'll watch your back, kid."

I looked up at the giant and fell to my knees. I kept remembering things in my past and felt my body weaken. The atmosphere around the tall being was draining me. I kept waking up in my past, it was showing me everything.

"Keep looking! There's gotta be more of 'em!" A voice called out. Footsteps sounded around me. I tried to look around, but I was concussed, something had just happened, something terrible. The sky above was grey, and I could smell gunpowder and blood.

"I don't think there's anyone left!" Another voice replied. I was fading in and out. I saw two men stepping around near where I was lying.

"I found one!" One of them called out. They had uniforms and weapons. Rebels. I remember The army had sent my unit to intercept them. Unfortunately, it seemed it didn't go as planned.

The two men dragged a soldier away. The wounded soldier had a blue uniform, like mine. I recognized the soldier that they were dragging away.

"Bill," I tried to say. I extended my hand, but I was pinned down by a mound of dirt and two dead soldiers from my unit.

I tried to speak louder, but I felt someone cover my mouth. I looked up to see a native standing above me. The native man held his finger over his lips, telling me to be quiet. I then felt him drag me away, and I began to blackout again.

I woke up by a fire. Two strangers sat by the flame, eating squirrels suspended above the flame. I was covered by a coat that looked like it once belonged to an animal.

"You're awake. That's good." one of the strangers spoke up as I looked around to see where I was.

"Who are you?" I asked, backing away.

The strangers didn't react. It seemed they didn't intend to kill me.

"Come and sit. Your body needs rest," the stranger continued.

"Who are you? Where am I?" I asked. "I need to get home. I can't stay here." I stood up to walk away, but I was pulled back by my waistline and fell to the ground.

"What the hell was that for?" I asked the stranger.

"You must eat. Your body is weakened from battle." The stranger replied.

I repositioned myself and sat by the fire.

"What happened to me?" I asked the native man I sat next to. He reached over the fire to take a chunk from the roasting squirrel.

"All of your men are dead." The native replied before biting into the crispy squirrel. The squishing of his teeth ripping the meat blared in my ears, and I remembered something.

"Where was Bill? Did you see what happened to him?" I asked, interrupting the native as he ate.

"What do you think?" the native muttered. He stood up, wiped his hands on a rag hanging from his waist, and walked over to a fur coat lying on the ground.

"Rest. Tomorrow, we can take you back to where you are from," The native laid down and fell asleep immediately. I looked at the other stranger sitting next to the fire. He hadn't said a word, and I still wanted to know why they had rescued me. I was about to ask him a question, but he shut his eyes and quickly went to sleep. I was left dumbfounded and unsure of what to do. I lay down next to the fire and fell asleep, too.

"Wake up," A voice sounded. My eyes opened to see the two natives preparing to head out. I stood up and picked up my coat.

"Where are we going?" I asked.

"Camp up north. Military, your side."

I paused before asking, "I need to know what happened to Bill," I confessed. The native seemed upset by my question.

"Why must you know the condition of Bill?" The native asked.

"I promised I would get him home," I replied.

The native groaned loudly and then turned to his companion to say something in their language. The other native simply nodded.

"Bison remembers where they took your friend. So he will take us there, but only to look."

"Okay. I just need to see if he's alive."

"My name is Ox," The native said in conclusion.

"I'm Aaron," I replied.

The natives nodded in agreement, and we went on our way.

"The hell is my goddamn uniform?" A voice called out. We had arrived at a rebel camp near the river. Ox took a telescope from his pack to scan the area for Bill. Ox let out a grunt and handed me the telescope. Ox then pointed his finger to where I should focus, and I looked through the telescope to see that the rebels had hung Bill from a tree with a sign that read, "Not free yet."

"Bastards!" I said, punching the ground.

Ox took the telescope and laid back, watching me react to what the rebels did to Bill, and he asked, "You made a promise to that boy?"

"I said I would protect him."

Ox looked at Bison to tell him something before looking back at me to say, "Come with us. We will gather warriors."

"Why?" I asked.

Ox stood up to leave and answered, "We will avenge your friend, Aaron."

I stood up quickly to follow Ox and Bison into the forest. I couldn't wait to bring hell to these animals.

My eyes opened up to see the giant being standing before me still. The creature spoke something into my ears, but I couldn't understand what it was saying. I felt only darkness. I closed my eyes and was in my memories again, deep in the forest, surrounded by a tribe of natives. The chief stood before me as they gathered around me. The chief invited me into his tent with Ox to protect me in battle before taking me back outside to a fire that the tribe had set up to dance to. I stood in front of the flame as the natives danced around me, chanting and singing. All I could feel inside me was anger and hatred, and I knew that all I wanted was vengeance. Then the night came.

We approached the camp silently. Twelve native warriors surrounded me as we crept up slowly to the rebel camp. Ox came to me and handed me a weapon, saying, "Here. This will protect you, Aaron."

We were now in the enemy's territory, creeping up to their tents to find them sleeping, silently taking their lives before the sunlight could touch their eyes. War cries echoed as the native warriors began pouring out of the woods, crossing the river to the camp. I fired my pistol and swung my hatchet, killing any rebel that was in my sight, their tents were set ablaze, and we burned their bodies with their weapons and made our exit. I took Bill's body and carried him to be buried. I placed him in a grave with Bill's army hat above it to mark where he rested. The natives surrounded me and helped me cover the hole before I dug another to bury my weapons and uniform, which I placed in a box that the natives crafted for me.

"There is darkness in you," a voice whispered. The giant reached out its hand, and I submerged in a black liquid that appeared beneath me. I sunk into the dark, reaching out until everything went black. I felt like I was drowning and shaking until I came out of the black fluid and fell onto the floor. The room was different now. I recognized it. I was lying on the floor in my bathroom. I had dropped out of the tub, covered in black fluid. A single light shined in the room, red like blood underneath the bathtub. I stood up and looked in the mirror to see myself, but nothing reflected on it, only darkness. I then heard a voice calling from downstairs. I ran down the corridor and hurried down the steps to find Jane standing in the living room.

"Jane?" I asked. She was dressed in white, like the last time I saw her.

"Aaron," Jane replied, smiling. "It's time to come home," she whispered.

I froze up. I couldn't believe she was here, standing before me again. I missed her so much.

"Jane....I can't," I whispered back. Tears formed in my eyes as Jane reached out to me.

"Please, Aaron." Jane's voice was filled with agony. I fell to my knees and cried. I knew she wasn't real. I looked behind her and saw Bill sitting in the chair in the corner. He didn't say anything, and his expression was blank. I felt my stomach sink to the floor, and my heart ached. I groaned loudly and screamed. I didn't know what to do. How could I escape this?

A light then filled the room with a warm glow as the curtains caught fire, setting the house ablaze. The chair Bill sat on was now on fire, and he sat in it, burning.

Jane's body erupted in flames, and she cried out, begging me to save her. I felt someone touch my shoulder, and I looked to see who was touching me before pulling my coat to look them in the eyes. A woman stood before me, grabbing onto me, screaming in my face, saying, "Remember me?" The woman was naked, with her body covered in gashes and bloody wounds. Her eyes were colored red, and her teeth were black with rot.

She slammed me against the wall and said, "You should've sent your angels to get me, little man! You think a little fire was going to stop me!"

I didn't know what to do. I was in shock. I didn't understand what was happening, and I watched as the demonic woman reached back her arm and began to strike, but we were both surprised by a blinding light that appeared in the living room. The flash of light disappeared quickly, and I woke up in the spirit house with Gabriel standing next to me.

"Well, look at that," Gabriel spoke up, "I thought I would never find you. Lucifer threw you in deep."

I looked up at Gabriel and asked, "What the hell was that?"

"That was your mind," Gabriel replied as he helped me.

"My mind is a fucked up place. I don't want to do that again. Ever."

"Don't worry, Aaron," Gabriel reassured. "We're almost done here. Let's go finish this, yeah?"

"Okay," I said nervously.

My vision blurred as I opened my eyes to see what was happening. Raphael was fighting Lucifer, and Gabriel exchanged blows with Asmodeus.

"Aaron," Gabriel's voice called out. "Touch the throne."

I looked at Lucifer's throne and could see black smoke coming from the seat. I reached out my hand and placed it against the black marble furniture and felt my blood rushing as my veins turned black. I couldn't hold on for very long as the power of the black throne was becoming too much for my body to take. I moved my hand away and stood up slowly. I noticed my gun lying on the floor next to the stairs. I picked it up and took my ax from my belt as I charged forward and swung it at Lucifer.

Lucifer noticed me sprinting towards him and ducked, dodging my attack. I quickly turned and swung again, but he deflected the attack and clashed his sword with my ax.

"So," Lucifer said, "you got a taste of my power."

I shook as he pressed harder and moved my other hand to reinforce my ax to keep him from cutting my face as I said to him, "I'm gonna kill you."

Lucifer grinned and pressed harder, forcing me back. He then moved the blade away and held onto my neck before throwing me across the room. I hit the floor and tried to stand up again, but I was paralyzed by Lucifer's hand as he whispered in my head, "You have my power flowing through your veins, but only I can control it."

I tried moving, but it was hurting me. I looked at Raphael and saw him charging Lucifer, but before he could strike, we were interrupted by a gunshot.

Raphael fell to the floor and held his hand against his leg as it began to bleed. I looked across the room and saw Leonard stepping out of the shadows with a gun in his hand. Asmodeus had appeared behind Raphael, landing a blow. Gabriel gripped the weapon out of Leonard's hand as Lucifer pointed his sword at Gabriel.

"Well done, Asmodeus," Lucifer said as Asmodeus approached to stand next to him. "Now, we can continue."

Asmodeus raised his staff to kill Raphael as Lucifer prepared to attack Gabriel. Then a blade burst out of Lucifer's chest as Asmodeus stood behind him as the weapon pierced Lucifer. Leonard charged at Asmodeus, but he was stopped as I fired my gun, hitting him in the chest. Leonard fell to the floor just after Lucifer. Asmodeus stepped around Lucifer, saying,

"I hope you're not surprised by this, Lucifer," Asmodeus said. "I've wanted this since we arrived here, and now you can finally feel the hatred of your brethren whom you have forced to serve you."

Asmodeus pulled on Lucifer's hair and forced him to the floor like an animal. I didn't know what to do. I was frozen, confused by what was happening. Then, finally, Gabriel appeared next to Raphael and healed his wound. Asmodeus looked at me and grinned as he waved his hand in the air, and we appeared on a grassy plain between a forest and a lake. I looked around and saw that everyone was still present.

"Asmodeus, you can't kill him!" Raphael exclaimed, rising to his feet.

Asmodeus didn't look at Raphael, but he grinned and said, "You wait your turn. I'm going to kill you right after."

Lucifer began to crawl away. I raised my gun to shoot Asmodeus, but all I got was the clicking sound of it being empty. I kept pulling the trigger, but nothing happened. Asmodeus grinned as he watched Lucifer crawl away like a wounded animal.

"You're going to die here," Asmodeus said, "and no one is going to know!"

Asmodeus fell silent, and the wind howled ominously. Finally, Asmodeus turned to the trees, and I could feel something approaching. A dark figure stepped out until I could finally see who it was.

"Astaroth," Lucifer hissed.

Astaroth approached the scene, dressed in black armor, carrying his massive sword and dragging it against the grass. The shadows of his legion stood behind him, hiding in the trees.

"I'm going to kill you both!" Lucifer screamed in anger before coughing up blood.

Astaroth appeared next to Gabriel and stuck him with his sword. Gabriel flew through the air, landing in the water. Astaroth then pinned Raphael to the ground with his boot, holding his sword next to Raphael's face, and smiled before moving closer to Lucifer. Asmodeus and Astaroth stood above Lucifer. They were going to kill him, but Raphael stood up and faced them before they did. Raphael's clothing was beginning to fade away, changing into armor. Raphael's armor was chrome and black, similar to theirs, but it was cleaner and had no damage or rust.

A wolf's head rested on his left shoulder, and he revealed his wings. Raphael breathed deeply and looked at them with intensity. He reached out his hand, and his sword flew to it.

Lucifer teleported away from Astaroth and headed toward the forest.

"Aaron!" Raphael called out. "Go after Lucifer!"

I quickly stood up and sprinted past Asmodeus and Astaroth. Astaroth moved his sword to strike me as I passed by, but his hand was stopped by Gabriel appearing before him.

I got away but was stopped by Leonard as he grabbed onto my heel and said, "Aaron, did she die peacefully?" Leonard asked. I didn't know who he was referring to at first.

"No," I said to him, remembering Rosier. "She's not resting peacefully either."

Leonard closed his eyes. He sniffled as he was beginning to cry. He took his gun and handed it to me. I knew what he wanted me to do. "Kill me," he whispered.

I took the gun and aimed it at his head as I said, pulling the trigger, "Burn in hell."

I looked back at Raphael and Gabriel, now dressed in armor, fighting the two demons. I turned around to the forest to see Astaroth's forces approaching. Gabriel appeared above me. I looked back to see that he was still fighting Astaroth. Gabriel was in two places at the same time.

"Aaron," Gabriel interrupted me, staring at his other self. "Follow Lucifer. Don't let him escape." Gabriel then flew up into the air and swung a massive sword that appeared in his hand, setting the forest on fire.

"Go, Aaron!" Gabriel instructed as he disappeared.

I hurried towards the forest in pursuit of Lucifer. I could see him in the distance. The forest burned around me, so I hustled to try to reach him, closing the gap between us. Lucifer was now within my grasp, but I couldn't touch him yet. As we approached a hill, I tackled Lucifer and we rolled down the hill. I kept my grip on his shirt as we tumbled down. We landed at the bottom but the forest had disappeared. I looked around us to see that we were in the place Lucifer had taken me to earlier or a place similar to it. I saw Lucifer running across the room, He climbed up on a statue shaped like the being I had seen in the nightmare that Lucifer placed me in. Lucifer stood at the edge of the giant's hands that were locked together as if they were praying. Lucifer looked down at me with his glowing, yellow irises and grinned. He stood naked in the hands of the statue. I stopped to see a massive cavity, a pool sitting under the tall structure.

Lucifer leaped forward and dunked himself in the pool. A long drop and then a splash, right into the red liquid that filled the cavity. I walked up to the large cavity to see what happened to Lucifer. The fluid stopped moving and I saw what looked like a massive skeleton floating up above the red liquid, the spine of a giant creature. The red fluid began to bubble and boil until a giant shot out of the pool, flying up and destroying the ceiling above, the hole left above revealed a church sitting above the massive, black room. The giant burst through the ceiling of the church, destroying the structure, and turning it into rubble. Then the giant stomped away.

I was left alone in the chamber. I didn't know what to do. "Gabriel!" I called out.

A brief silence, then an answer.

"What is it, Aaron?" Gabriel's voice appeared.

"There might be something coming your way."

"What? Do you know what it is?" Gabriel questioned.

"I think it's Lucifer," I replied.

MORNINGSTAR

Raphael

"Time to die!" Asmodeus screamed as Gabriel and I stood ready to attack again. Asmodeus leaped into the air and slammed his staff against the ground as he descended. The earth shook and split apart, rising as the shockwave moved towards us. Gabriel and I flew up into the air. Asmodeus and Astaroth moved closer to us, using the rubble as footing to gain height. They leaped across the rubble, getting closer. I flew towards Asmodeus, taking him mid-flight and throwing him down to the ground; Asmodeus crashed through the rubble, descending onto the water below. I kept striking him with speed and precision until he hit the water, and I flew in to subdue Asmodeus, placing a seal on his chest. Chains appeared, wrapping Asmodeus until he couldn't move, and he sunk into the lake, down into the dark of the waters.

I flew back up to the surface and looked at the forest, hearing loud booms, and watched as the forest's trees shook and fell. Something was coming. The cracks grew louder and louder until finally, the forest opened, and a massive creature burst out of the trees. The giant slammed a black sword into the lake, creating a gigantic wave. The water flowed into the surrounding forest, flooding the terrain. I looked at Gabriel, standing next to Astaroth as they stood on the water, watching the giant approach.

"Contain it!" I shouted to Gabriel, but he didn't hear me. "Gabriel!" I called out. He finally turned to look at me as the giant had disappeared. Gabriel looked surprised. He pointed his finger and said,

"Watch out!"

I turned to see that the giant had appeared behind me. It had teleported. A massive hand approached me, and I couldn't dodge it in time. The giant flung me across the lake into a mountain. I smashed through trees, slamming into the rocky surface. I lay on the ground, looking at the sky above. Drops of moisture started to appear. The clouds turned darker, and thunder began to form. I stood off the ground and looked across the ridge, spotting the giant. Astaroth began to attack the creature as Gabriel flew up into the sky, high above them.

Gabriel's sword flashed with a bright glow, and the earth shook violently. The clouds opened, revealing seven massive beings standing taller than the mountains. Gabriel pointed his sword down and teleported back down to the water.

Gabriel stood before the giant. Astaroth was still attacking the creature. Gabriel opened his hand, putting his palm forward in the creature's direction. Astaroth leaped in the air to attack, Stabbing his sword into the giant's chest. The blade pierced the creature, impaling it. Astaroth held onto his sword but was grabbed by the giant to be thrown away. Then suddenly, A massive, gold sword pierced the giant's hand, stabbing Astaroth. A giant chain was attached to the blade, shining gold with demon blood dripping from the edge. More appeared in the distance, gold blades attached to chains flying toward Lucifer's creature. Finally, seven golden swords punctured the giant's body, pinning it to the ground and disabling the creature's movement. The giant roared with anger, struggling to break free.

Astaroth cried out in anger, now stuck to the giant's chest with a sword impaled on his back. I reached out my hand to form a tall spear with a hook at the end—the leviathan spear. I gripped the weapon and raised it in the air. Lightning struck the spear, making the spear longer.

Lightning coursed through my armor and my body, and I flew up into the air, taking the spear. I teleported down to the water where the giant was. Lightning flashed around the giant, and the massive beings around us pulled on the chains holding the giant down. The creature flapped its great, black wings. Gabriel placed his sword against the water, creating a dome over the creature that kept it from going up into the air. The giant slammed against the golden energy field. Gabriel held his sword tightly, attempting to contain the giant under the shield. The giant pushed against the energy field until finally, Gabriel released the energy, and the area disappeared. The tall beings surrounding us were gone too, and the swords attached to chains no longer glowed.

The giant took to the sky, but it hadn't noticed that I was approaching, and right before the giant took flight, I descended onto it, pushing the spear against the metal spike covering the giant's face, shattering the massive, metal structure. The spear punctured the giant's forehead in a gigantic black eye that sat above two eyes just like it. The giant's blood shot out like a geyser as the spear dug deeper into its skull. The spear was now deep in the giant's head, and I let go of it. The giant began to fall back, but just before it did, a flash of lightning struck its head, passing through and hitting the ground beneath. The lightning bolt burned a hole into the giant's eye as its corpse collapsed onto the forest.

I touched down onto the water next to Gabriel. The giant laid dead before us.

"It seems we are done here," Gabriel spoke up.

I didn't say anything before flying up in the air to see Astaroth lying dead. I landed near Astaroth's corpse and approached, but I stopped when Asmodeus appeared, coming out of a portal. He sprinted in my direction but was looking back at something, and then I saw Aaron, stepping out of the doorway with a gun in his hand, aimed at Asmodeus' back, firing three shots. Asmodeus fell forward, landing right in front of me.

DEVILS

Aaron

I looked for an exit out of the chamber and saw the massive doors at the end of the room. I walked in the direction of the entrance until I heard the doors opening. I reached for the gun I had on me and aimed. A hand crept out from behind the doors before I saw a group of children entering the chamber. I lowered the weapon and walked toward the kids, saying, "It's all right. I'm going to get you out of here."

The kids all stayed quiet as I approached. I reached out my hand, stepping closer, and just as I was putting the pistol away, a man yelled from across the room. I turned to find Asmodeus falling out of a portal. Water poured out from the doorway as Asmodeus plopped onto the chamber floor, wet and nearly drowning with chains wrapped around him. Asmodeus coughed and choked, rolling over on the floor. It seemed he didn't know where he was, and he hadn't noticed me yet. I stood up slowly, taking the gun in my hand to cock back the hammer, slowly raising it to aim at Asmodeus.

"I know you're here, Aaron," Asmodeus spoke up after taking a breath. He sat up and dipped his head, sitting still on the floor. I walked up slowly, keeping his head in my crosshairs. Asmodeus chuckled and looked up at me to say something.

"You have got to be the most unfortunate thing I've ever seen."

Asmodeus leaned forward until he fell and his head hit the floor. He moved his legs to get on his knees. Asmodeus rose slowly, his yellow eyes piercing through his drooping hair.

"You are supposed to be dead, Aaron," Asmodeus whispered. "Did you think you would end up in this position at the moment of your death?" Asmodeus whipped his hair out of the way to look me in the eye. I hadn't answered his question. Asmodeus chuckled as I crept closer.

"They always find a way, don't they?" Asmodeus asked. He was referring to Gabriel and Raphael. I was done listening to Asmodeus' rambling. I prepared to fire the gun to kill Asmodeus, saying, "you sent me to hell when you took Jane, and you killing me kept me from suffering, but because of what you are, I needed to fight again. You are evil, Asmodeus, an evil that cannot be stopped, and I'm just a dead man."

Asmodeus grinned, looking across the room. I turned to see he was looking at the staff on the floor. I turned back to Asmodeus when I heard him sprinting in my direction. I pulled the gun's trigger but missed when Asmodeus tackled me to the floor. The gun fell out of my hand as we both tumbled to the floor. I got up quickly and took my hatchet to attack. Asmodeus lunged at me, and I ducked. He sprinted past, just missing me. His jaw snapped as he tried biting into my arm. I swung the ax, hitting his leg, and pulled on it, flipping Asmodeus before he slammed onto the floor. I swung the ax down at Asmodeus, but he rolled away and kicked me, sending me flying across the floor.

Asmodeus rolled, took the staff behind his back, and squatted down to touch the floor with the staff. I quickly moved to grab the gun and fired. The bullet hit Asmodeus in the back, and he was pushed into a portal, leaving the staff behind. I put Leonard's gun in my holster and ran over to where the doorway was, but it was gone. I then looked at the weapon and picked it up. I took it with both hands and touched the floor with it. The orb on the bottom end glowed and opened a portal to where Raphael and Gabriel were. Asmodeus was running to them, and he turned back to look at me as I dropped the staff and took my gun from my belt, aiming at Asmodeus to fire three shots into his back.

I stepped out of the portal to see Asmodeus kneeling before Raphael, pressing on the wounds I had given him. Astaroth lay dead on the ground next to them. Asmodeus looked up at Raphael. He breathed heavily, screaming with anger as he said, "You don't know what you just did!"

Raphael hid his wings and approached Asmodeus.

"You will not get what you want, Asmodeus," Raphael said. "You will not have my mercy."

Asmodeus shook with rage. He kneeled upright, keeping his eyes on Raphael as he said, "I... don't... want your mercy!"

I tensed up and watched as Asmodeus stood up and charged Raphael. Gabriel prepared to attack, and so did Raphael, but just before Asmodeus could reach certain destruction, a hand burst out from underneath him, out of the giant. A bloodied Lucifer erupted from the giant's flesh, taking Asmodeus by the neck. A man of pale skin and blackened hands with wings like a dragon. Two beading, black eyes with two more sitting close to his temples and two black horns resting on his head. I could hear flesh tearing as Lucifer tightened his grip on Asmodeus' neck. Finally, Lucifer spoke in a demonic voice, saying to Asmodeus, "Die, my humble servant. Die with my hand squeezing your beating heart."

Raphael revealed his wings as he and Gabriel took flight towards Lucifer. I took Leonard's gun and saw that it had one bullet left in the cylinder. I cocked back the hammer and aimed at Asmodeus. Lucifer reached back with his right arm and struck Asmodeus in the chest. Lucifer's hand penetrated the torso through, gripping Asmodeus' heart and ripping it from his chest. Lucifer slid his hand out, leaving a hole in Asmodeus' body. Lucifer looked through the gaping hole to see me as I fired Leonard's gun and watched the bullet pass through the wound and hit Lucifer in the head. The round ripped apart the horn on his right side, and he fell back and stopped moving.

Raphael looked surprised by what had just happened, stopping before Lucifer as he collapsed to the ground. I shook nervously, but my hand was still, holding onto the gun. I still couldn't believe what just happened was real. Lucifer began to move, and I stepped forward, reloading Leonard's pistol, but Raphael signaled me to stop.

"Gabriel!" Raphael shouted.

Gabriel took flight, splitting into two, swooping down to pin Lucifer to the ground. Raphael swept his hand against his sword, igniting it with a black flame. Raphael leaped forward and pushed the sword into Lucifer's chest. Lucifer struggled to break free of Gabriel's hold, screaming with rage as Raphael shoved the blade deeper. I stood frozen, seeing what was happening. Lucifer shook violently and cursed Raphael and Gabriel for what they were doing. Lucifer then looked at me and motioned his fingers, making my right arm move to fire Leonard's gun. I tried to stop myself but pulled the trigger, and the bullet hit Gabriel's clone, making it disappear before Lucifer raised his arm to prevent Raphael's sword from going deeper. Gabriel pushed Lucifer down by the neck, but he started pulling the sword out of his chest. The blade slid out slowly as Raphael fought to keep it in Lucifer. I kneeled, held onto my right arm, and forced my fingers to stop gripping the gun until it fell out of my hand, and I noticed that my veins had turned black again. Lucifer's power was still flowing through me.

"You cannot contain me," Lucifer said to Gabriel and Raphael. "I've been set free!"

I looked up when I heard Raphael's sword snapping in half. Lucifer kicked Raphael back and swung his arm at Gabriel. Lucifer pressed against the energy field surrounding Gabriel until his hand broke through, and Gabriel rolled around out of the way. Lucifer then flew up into the sky as a lightning bolt struck him, and he vanished, leaving us in silence.

Raphael kneeled on the ground, staring at the broken hilt of his sword. Asmodeus and Astaroth's corpses began rotting and melting away until they were nothing but smoke. Raphael stood up and looked at the giant's corpse as it deteriorated.

"Gabriel, grab Aaron," Raphael shouted, "The corpse is beginning to rot!"

Gabriel swooped me up from off the giant's corpse as he and Raphael flew down to the grass by the water. Gabriel set me down and walked to the edge of the lake where Raphael was standing, looking out into the water as the giant melted away.

"It seems it's not over," Gabriel stated.

"No...." Raphael replied, "It is not."

Gabriel fell silent and turned to me before saying, "Well, let's head back then. There's nothing left to do here."

We all stood in silence. Before I spoke up, saying, "There's one more thing."

Raphael opened a portal to where I found the statue of Lucifer's giant. The children I had seen were still there, waiting, sitting on the steps of the entrance to the massive room. The light of the broken ceiling pierced through into the dark.

"It's not unlike them to use children as slaves or worse," Raphael said with disdain.

Gabriel patted Raphael's shoulder, saying, "I know, Raphael." Gabriel then approached the group of children and instructed them to follow him into a portal.

"Where's he taking them?" I asked Raphael.

"To a safe place," Raphael replied. "Let's go, Aaron. This place is going to collapse into a dimension of darkness very soon. You don't want to be here when that happens."

We arrived at the spirit house. I sat at the library table and put my feet up.

"So, what now?" I asked.

"It's time for you to go home," Gabriel said, appearing in the library.

"I hadn't thought about that," I said. "What's gonna happen to me?"

"Come with me," Gabriel said.

I stood up from my chair and followed Gabriel out of the room, but before I walked out, I stopped as Raphael called to me, nodding his head in approval, saying, "I hope you find peace now, Aaron. Thank you."

"Thanks for giving me a chance to do something right," I replied before walking out to follow Gabriel as I closed the door.

Gabriel walked me through the main hallway to a room at the end. He stopped at the door and said to me,

"Aaron, you did well. We could not have accomplished this without you. Thank you for your helping us." Gabriel smiled and opened the door to let me in.

I walked up and stopped to ask, "what about Lucifer?"

Gabriel sighed.

"Well, it seems we're still hunting him, but don't worry. We've weakened his forces, and with him staying in the physical realm, he won't have many places to hide. We'll find him, Aaron. I promise you."

I nodded.

"Let's get you home, yeah?" Gabriel chirped, breaking the silence.

"Yeah," I said somberly and walked into the darkness. I walked until I saw the light floating in front of me. I approached the morning, and it spoke to me.

"Welcome!" A voice said enthusiastically. It sounded like a small child.

"We've been expecting you!" The voice continued, "Someone will be with you shortly."

I stepped back and stood there waiting. Nothing was happening, and I was becoming anxious. I turned away from the light and closed my eyes, unsure of what would happen. Then I opened them to see that I was surrounded by white. I looked around, trying to figure out where I was. My eyes rushed about, looking for a sign, but I stopped when I heard someone speaking. Standing near a river, I looked back and found myself in the woods. A wooden boat floated in the water with one passenger.

"Jane," I whispered.

Jane removed the cloak covering her face, and she told me to get in the water as she stepped off the boat into the river. I stepped forward, letting the river consume me as I grew closer to Jane, now making her way towards me until I reached her and held her tightly. My eyes filled with tears, and I kissed Jane, closing my eyes. The water rushed around us, but I knew I was home and waited, never to open my eyes again.

LEGION

Jim Lucas
Chicago, 1972

"I've never seen anything like it," the mortician's voice echoed in the hallway of the old morgue. I took a long drag from my cigarette and put it out before placing it in my pocket as the mortician explained what was odd about these corpses. I was there to look at a number of victims all left in similar conditions. A janitor that worked at an executive plaza downtown, a mother of two that worked in a convenience store down the road from the plaza, and two teenagers around age 18, were all killed in a brutal fashion but their bodies were still intact, just the skin, and their bones, but all of their organs had been removed.

"What's this?" I asked Lupe, the mortician. I pressed my hand against the symbol that was branded on one of the victims, A star with five points surrounded by a circle.

"Appears to be some sort of brand," Lupe acknowledged. "I've seen them on a couple of the other bodies that have been coming in. It's getting rough out there, 'mano."

"The star's pointed downward," I pointed out. "Does that mean something?"

Lupe removed his arm from the cart that carried his paperwork. "I have no idea," he said. "I just take them in and book them. I don't really worry about what happened to them out there. That's...."

"-My job," I said, cutting him off.

"Yeah," Lupe said, nodding awkwardly. "I'm not proud of this job but it pays the bill, compa'."

Lupe slid the corpses back into their mortuary cabinets and I looked at the brand on the corpse I was standing by.

"I hope you coming here was useful to your investigation, detective," Lupe concluded. "I have to start booking them and notify the families."

I jotted down the information into my notes, telling Lupe, "It's good enough. Call me if you find any more. I'll have some officers form a perimeter around this area, this could be the work of a serial killer."

"Oh, yeah, I've heard of those. That's fucked up," Lupe added.

"Yeah, it's horrible. Well, keep me posted, Lupe, so I can find whoever did this."

"Yeah, you got it, Jim. Good luck. Oh, and say hello to your auntie for me. I'll be swinging by to buy some of her cookies. Those little pastries are addictive 'mano."

I reached for the doorknob and told Lupe to lay off the sweets, which made me look stupid considering I had just finished an entire cigarette. "You gotta watch those calories. You'll end up on one of those slabs," I said.

"Fuck, it bro. You only live once. You gotta enjoy the sweet stuff," Lupe said, chuckling as he slid the last two bodies into the cabinet.

I nodded and agreed with Lupe, "You ain't wrong, brother." I said, making my way out into the hallway about to close the door behind me when I heard a loud clanging down the hall. I looked at Lupe and he shrugged and nodded his head, saying there shouldn't be anyone else in the building.

I took my pistol out of my shoulder holster and told Lupe to stay put. I held the weapon out in front of me as I walked down the hall, trying to listen for more movement. The hallway was dark, all of the lights had been turned off since no one was supposed to be working except for Lupe. Who comes to a morgue at two in the morning? I thought. It might've been local punks or maybe a suspect trying to erase evidence, possibly here to hurt Lupe to keep the information from being recorded, either way, I had to go see.

I made my way down the long, dark hall and started seeing footprints on the floor when I pulled out my flashlight. The footprints showed that the intruder was barefoot, which I found odd but what bothered me was that the footprints were left with blood. If this was the killer, then I had to find them, and if it wasn't, then I hoped they weren't here to hurt anyone, I'd had enough stressful things going on today.

I followed the bloody footprints to the upper level of the building, going further up until I reached the roof access. The door leading outside had been left open. I could hear the sound of pouring rain coming in, wetting the floor of the exit. I stepped outside and scanned the area with my weapon in case of a threat and I looked across to the other side of the roof and saw someone standing, naked in the rain. I thought they were crazy for standing outside in the freezing rain like this, which made me more cautious when approaching the mysterious, naked man.

"Chicago P.D!" put your hand in the air. Show me you're not armed!" I called out. The stranger did as I said. "Turn and face me! Do not lower your arms!"

The stranger turned to face me and noticed something familiar about him. It was a young man that I had seen before. Then it hit me. This boy was one of the victims Lupe had shown me but why was he here and alive?

The young man started crying, saying he didn't know where he was. He kept saying he wanted to go home. I told him to calm down but he started to panic. His movements became more uncomfortable and I kept telling him to relax, but he turned around suddenly and ran to the edge of the roof before jumping off. I sprinted to him to try and stop him but he was gone and I looked down at the street and saw nothing, not even his body, and I was left alone in the rain.

I hurried down the hall and saw Lupe standing outside of the morgue.

"What was it?" Lupe asked.

"Just some punks trying to get a look at a dead body," I answered, walking past Lupe, and making my way to the exit.

"Okay," Lupe said, "Well, good luck on the investigation!"

"Thanks!" I said, walking to the end of the hall. "Call me if more turn up!" I took the turn at the end of the hall and exited out to the side of the building to get in my car. The rain was hammering down and I could barely see outside. I switched on the engine and turned on the headlights before driving away. I drove through the city, making my way home. It was late so there weren't many people around and I tried to turn on the radio but kept getting static. I kept my attention on the radio's panel and fiddled with it but had no luck.

I then smacked the radio hard until music came on but by then I hadn't been paying attention to the road and I drove right into something that appeared in front of the car. I jolted forward as the car stopped in its tracks and hit the steering wheel, dazing me. I rose up slowly, pressing my forehead, groaning loudly as I looked up to see what I had hit but there was nothing on the road except for street lamps. I sat back and looked up, rubbing my head. I had to go see what I crashed into, so I opened the car door and stepped out into the rain.

I stepped in front of the car, the headlights showing what was in front but I found nothing except the road. I looked at the car and found my front bumper was dented. I walked into the grassy field, next to the car, pointing my flashlight to the ground to see if something had fallen or was thrown by the car's impact but found nothing.

Then the street lamps flickered until they began to turn off. One by one, each lamp turned off and I ran back to the car right before the lamp above my car shut off too. I turned on the interior lights of the car as the headlights had shut off, too. Then I heard what sound like someone walking on top of the car. Footsteps thumped against the roof of the car and then it stopped. The interior lights flicked until they burned out and I took my flashlight. I locked the doors and scanned the darkness to see what was outside. Then the car rumbled on my side when it was hit by something. Then the other side. The car started to shake and move violently. Something bashed the windows like fists, but the flashlight showed nothing. I thought the windows were about to shatter but then a light appeared down the road. A set of headlights blinded me, and the shadow of a deformed creature appeared in front of my car, a human body but the neck was elongated and the head connected to it floated above like a haunting caricature.

"What the f..."

A booming sound made me duck behind the seat. But I looked to see that the weird figure just got its head blown off. The creature fell back as another round hit its stomach. The silhouette of the person firing appeared in the headlamps of the car on the road. The stranger walked up and placed another shell in the creature's chest. The creature stopped moving and the stranger walked away. I hurried out of the car and aimed my gun at the stranger.

"Chicago PD! Drop the gun, shithead!" I yelled at the stranger and they stopped walking.

"You better have a permit for that weapon!" I yelled, "and you better not be out here murdering people! Drop the shotgun!"

The stranger opened his car door.

"Hey!" I yelled as the stranger threw the gun in his car and turned around.

"That wasn't a person, detective," the stranger said back. I stepped forward to look at what he was firing at and saw the grotesque creature lying dead on the ground. A foul smell came from the corpse and it was shaped exactly as I had seen. A human body with an elongated neck. I didn't know what the hell I was staring at. I heard a car door closing shut and saw the stranger driving away.

"Stop!" I yelled, taking aim with my pistol to fire two shots as he sped off into the dark. The street lamps turned on again and I ran back to my car to follow the mysterious driver. I tried turning the car on but had no luck. I kept trying but the engine didn't do anything. I smacked the steering wheel, saying, "Come on, you piece of old, rusty shit!" Then the car turned on by itself and I screamed, "Yes! I knew wouldn't let me down, baby!" I put the car in gear and dove down the road until I reached the neighborhood I lived in, still looking for the mysterious stranger but I couldn't find him so I gave up and headed home.

Lightning Source UK Ltd.
Milton Keynes UK
UKHW010136110223
416836UK00003B/97